Her little son wa~~s absolutely~~ perfect...

"He's zonked. Our Ethan's a great little sleeper."

Our Ethan. A fresh wave of confused longing rose up in Natalie, painful feelings she had no idea what to do with.

"You've been sleeping pretty well yourself." Jacob smiled at her. "I'm glad. You earned it."

"You must be pretty exhausted, too."

Dark circles shadowed his eyes, but when their glances met, he offered her another easy smile.

"Don't worry about me. Not the first night I've spent at the hospital. Besides, I had the easy job." His tired smile widened. "You were the superhero."

"Not me." Natalie shook her head. "I was scared to death."

"That's what makes it amazing. You pushed through the fear and pain with everything you had. It was one of the bravest things I've ever seen. Nope," he said as Natalie started to speak. "No arguing. I was there. I saw it. Give yourself some credit, Natalie. You're way stronger than you seem to think."

Laurel Blount lives on a small farm in Middle Georgia with her husband, David, their four children, a milk cow, dairy goats, assorted chickens, an enormous dog, three spoiled cats and one extremely bossy goose with boundary issues. She divides her time between farm chores, homeschooling and writing, and she's happiest with a cup of steaming tea at her elbow and a good book in her hand.

Books by Laurel Blount

Love Inspired

A Family for the Farmer
A Baby for the Minister

A Baby
for the Minister

Laurel Blount

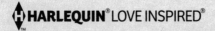

 LOVE INSPIRED BOOKS

Recycling programs
for this product may
not exist in your area.

ISBN-13: 978-1-335-42833-2

A Baby for the Minister

Copyright © 2018 by Laurel Blount

All rights reserved. Except for use in any review, the reproduction
or utilization of this work in whole or in part in any form by any
electronic, mechanical or other means, now known or hereafter
invented, including xerography, photocopying and recording, or in
any information storage or retrieval system, is forbidden without
the written permission of the editorial office, Love Inspired Books,
195 Broadway, New York, NY 10007 U.S.A.

This is a work of fiction. Names, characters, places and incidents are
either the product of the author's imagination or are used fictitiously, and
any resemblance to actual persons, living or dead, business establishments,
events or locales is entirely coincidental.

This edition published by arrangement with Love Inspired Books.

® and TM are trademarks of Love Inspired Books, used under license.
Trademarks indicated with ® are registered in the United States Patent
and Trademark Office, the Canadian Intellectual Property Office and in
other countries.

www.Harlequin.com

Printed in U.S.A.

For, lo, the winter is past, the rain is over
and gone; The flowers appear on the earth;
the time of the singing of birds is come, and the
voice of the turtle is heard in our land.
—*Song of Solomon* 2:11–12

For my beloved parents-in-law,
Lamont and Annette Blount, whose kindness,
integrity and strength bless all who know them,
and whose real-life love story is more inspiring
than any I could ever write.

Chapter One

Pastor Jacob Stone strode down the carpeted halls of the unfamiliar church, hoping he was headed in the right direction. He'd told the nervous bridegroom he'd be back in five minutes, and he was way past that deadline now. "My notes for the budget meeting are in the blue folder, Arlene. Keep looking."

"Good gracious, Jacob, this desk is like a landfill." He could hear rustling through his cell phone as his elderly secretary rummaged through stacks of paper. "No wonder you can't keep track of anything. Okay, I've found the folder. What am I supposed to do with it?"

"Make copies and take them to the conference room." Jacob checked his watch. "Then just sit in for me until I get there. I shouldn't be more than twenty minutes late. Twenty-five, tops."

"*Five* minutes late would be too much." Arlene made a *tsking* sound. "You're already on thin ice with Digby Markham because you skipped out on his businessmen's luncheon last week. I really don't see why you agreed to do this wedding. It's not even at our church."

"I told you—it was a last-minute thing. Pastor Michaelson came down with the flu." Jacob halted in front of the third door on the left. He was almost sure this was where he'd left the groom.

"Yes, but I don't see why Good Shepherd's emergency is our problem, especially when you already had Digby's meeting on the calendar. You need to start saying no."

"We're talking about somebody's *wedding*, Arlene. I couldn't say no."

Well, he could have. He just hadn't wanted to.

From the moment Digby had taken over as the chairman of Pine Valley Community Church's board, the banker had been clogging Jacob's schedule with endless meetings, all of which circled back to the same old topic: whether or not their little church should construct a fancy new fellowship hall.

Jacob already knew his answer to that question, and he was tired of arguing the same points over and over. A last-minute wedding made a welcome change.

Arlene sighed. "You really need to watch your

step right now, Jacob. The whole church is up in arms, and people are choosing sides. Digby might be a frustrating old fusspot, but plenty of folks are backing him up on this."

"We don't need a new fellowship hall. There are way too many genuine needs in our community for us to waste money on a new building when the space we already have is perfectly—"

"Adequate." Arlene finished the sentence with him. "So you've said. But it may surprise you to know that there are a good many people in our church who don't agree with your ideas of what's *adequate*."

No, that didn't surprise him. But it worried him. His church was pretty much the only family he had. He didn't like being on the outs with them. Still, it was his job to make the right decisions, not the popular ones.

"I don't think it sends the right message for us to fundraise right now. Since the textile plant shut down, half our town is out of work. We can talk about a new fellowship hall later, when our neighbors aren't worried about losing their homes."

"I'm already on your side, so you can save your breath. But I'll tell you this—a lot of people with some serious social clout want this fellowship hall to go forward. If you don't let them have it, you stand a good chance of losing your pulpit."

His cranky secretary actually sounded worried. "Aw. Would you miss me, Arlene?"

She snorted. "Don't you flatter yourself. I'm just too old to train up another new preacher. Now, enough of this jibber-jabber. You'd best get that couple married and get back here where you belong."

Jacob sighed as he slipped his phone back into his pocket. Arlene was right. He needed to get back to Pine Valley Community as soon as he could.

First, though, he had a wedding to perform and a spooked groom to deal with.

He needed to focus. Jacob closed his eyes and murmured a prayer.

Then he sucked in a deep breath, fixed a smile on his face and pushed open the door to the choir room.

"All right! Let's get this show on the…"

He froze, the rest of his cheery speech forgotten as he took in the scene in front of him.

Long gray curtains rippled as a chilly April breeze blew through the open window, filling the room with the smell of pine trees and wet asphalt. A crushed white boutonniere lay discarded on the carpet. The groom… What was his name again?

Adam Larkey.

Adam was nowhere to be seen.

Jacob's heart gave one slow, painful thump, then revved into high gear. He crossed the room in two strides and batted the fluttering curtains aside to scan the damp parking lot. Sure enough, a bumper-sticker-encrusted Jeep that he'd noticed earlier had vanished, replaced by a rectangle of dry pavement.

Oh brother. This was bad.

Really, really bad.

The ceremony was due to start in exactly eight minutes, and Elvis had left the building.

He'd never had anybody actually bolt from a wedding before. This was uncharted territory.

Oh, he'd dealt with panicky grooms plenty of times. What minister hadn't? That was why, when the first words out of Adam Larkey's mouth had been "I don't think I can do this, bro," Jacob hadn't taken it all that seriously.

Apparently, he should have.

He hadn't believed for a minute that Larkey was serious about skipping out. Grooms never were, not really.

And there was no way Jacob could've suspected that this guy would be the world's one exception because Jacob had never met either member of this wedding party before.

In fact, he still hadn't laid eyes on the bride.

He'd skidded into the church only a scant half hour before the wedding was scheduled to start. Since then he'd been so busy coping with Adam and Arlene that he hadn't had time to speak with the bride.

Well, he was definitely going to have to go talk to her now. He checked his watch again and winced. Zero hour.

There was no way around it. He had to go tell some poor woman that her fiancé had just climbed out of a window rather than marry her.

This was not going to be fun.

Jacob threaded his way back through the narrow halls toward the bride's dressing room, racking his brain for the best way to break the news. Unfortunately, Good Shepherd Church wasn't much bigger than his own, and he was standing outside the door before he came up with anything useful.

He spread his hand flat against the wood of the door and bowed his head. *Please, Lord. Help me to find the best words to explain this mess. Help this woman, whoever she is, to handle what I'm about to tell her with the kind of grace and peace only You can give. Carry her through this disappointment, Father, and heal her heart. Amen.*

As if on cue, the door opened a crack, and

Jacob found himself looking down into a woman's wide brown eyes.

"Is it time?"

Her voice wobbled as she tucked loosened strands of maple-sugar hair back into a softly coiled bun. She wore no veil, and Jacob had seen enough brides to know that the simple hairdo and light makeup were her own work. Not surprising, since this was supposed to be a no-frills wedding.

He forced a smile and extended his hand through the cracked door. "I'm Pastor Jacob Stone from Pine Valley Community Church. I'm pinch-hitting for Pastor Michaelson today."

"Oh! It's nice to meet you." The woman accepted his hand, her fingers icy in his. "I'm Natalie Davis. Are you ready for me now?"

"Not exactly. There's been a small…uh… glitch." As soon as the words were out of his mouth, he cringed. *A small glitch?*

"Another one?" Natalie laughed nervously. "First my car wouldn't start, then the minister gets sick and now this. I'm starting to wonder if this wedding is even going to happen today."

"May I come in? We need to talk."

The bride's creamy skin went a shade paler. "All right. Come on in and have a seat." Pulling the door open wide, she turned sideways, making room for him to enter.

Jacob didn't budge. For the second time that afternoon, he found himself frozen on a threshold with no clue what to do next.

He'd thought this wedding couldn't get any more complicated. He'd been wrong.

In the back of his bewildered mind at least a hundred alarm bells were going off at once. He had no idea what to say. In fact, at that moment, he knew only three things for certain.

First, there was no way he was making it to that meeting. Arlene would just have to cope with Digby and the board on her own.

And second, he should definitely have taken Adam Larkey's prewedding freak-out a whole lot more seriously.

Because the third thing he knew for sure was—that wasn't a bridal gown Natalie Davis was wearing.

It was a maternity dress.

"You're *pregnant*?" He didn't know why he made it sound like a question. With a baby bump of that size, there was absolutely no doubt about it.

Natalie's cheeks were stinging so hard that she knew they must be as red as apples, but she forced a little laugh. "Eight months and counting. Please. Come on in"

She made her way back to the worn armchair,

her Bible lying open on its seat. A few more minutes and one short ceremony and she could get out of this church and stop blushing every time somebody mentioned her pregnancy. She wasn't sure which of those two things she was looking forward to more.

It was hard being a new Christian when your past mistakes were so obvious.

She picked up the book and lowered herself gingerly back into the chair. She was glad she'd brought her Bible with her. Changing into her nicest maternity dress hadn't taken very long, and as the hour of her wedding approached, she'd grown more and more nervous.

She'd seen the quick, sidelong glances as she'd hurried down the hallway to this room. It certainly wasn't the first time church ladies had looked down their noses at her, but today, with her nerves already jumping, it was all a little too much. So she'd turned to the Psalms, hoping to find some peace.

The Bible was still pretty unfamiliar territory, but whispering the calming verses aloud had helped her settle down. Unfortunately, the serious look on this handsome minister's face was stirring all her butterflies right back up again.

He lingered in the doorway for a second. When he finally did come over to claim the empty chair, his leg brushed hers and she caught a whiff of spicy, masculine soap. She scooted a little farther away, wishing their seats weren't quite so close together.

This man sure didn't look like any preacher she'd ever seen before. He was way too good-looking, for one thing. As if being born with golden hair and sea-blue eyes wasn't enough, he also sported a strong square chin and broad, quarterback shoulders.

He was watching her silently, drumming his fingers on his knees.

"You look like you've had the wind knocked out of you, Pastor. I'm guessing nobody told you about my…condition?"

The minister cleared his throat. "No, I'm afraid not."

Not this again. Old Pastor Michaelson had only agreed to marry them after a long and embarrassing lecture. She wasn't sure she could take another one of those, not right now. "Do you have a problem performing the ceremony? Because I'm pregnant, I mean?"

This was exactly why she'd lobbied for a courthouse wedding. She'd been getting this kind of reaction from people ever since the day she'd had to change into maternity clothes. If she hadn't needed her new faith so desperately, she might have given up on religion altogether.

As it was, she'd just given up on churches.

But this man immediately shook his head.

"No! Not at all." The denial came out with such force that Natalie actually believed him. "Sorry, it's just…there's no easy way to say this." The minister took a deep breath and looked at her directly. She braced herself.

"What?"

"Adam has had some…uh…second thoughts."

"Second thoughts?" Natalie blinked. That was the reason for all this?

She'd had a few second thoughts of her own. But in the end she always came back to the same hard truth.

Marrying Adam was the right thing to do.

"But isn't that pretty normal?" she asked. *Especially for a man who'd basically been strong-armed by his grandmother into getting married in the first place.*

She kept that last bit to herself. There was no need for everybody to know that the father of her baby had needed an awful lot of convincing to marry her. This situation was already humiliating enough.

"It's totally normal, but I'm afraid this is more serious than an ordinary case of cold feet." He paused. "I'm so sorry."

Natalie's heart fell. He was *so sorry*. That could only mean one thing.

The wedding was off.

She could feel him watching her, obviously braced for some kind of explosion. Well, he was wasting his time. She was way too exhausted for anything like that.

Instead, she just blinked at the burgundy carpet, her still-new Bible pressed against the bulge of her pregnant tummy, her brain struggling to catch up.

Could this really be happening? After all the praying, all the planning… Adam was dumping her here at the last possible minute? Seriously?

What on earth was she going to do now?

"Natalie? Could I go out to the sanctuary and get somebody for you? Your mom? A sister, maybe?"

She brought her gaze back to his face. "No," she managed. "There's nobody. I don't actually…have much family."

The worry in his eyes morphed into a compassion so warm that she had to fight a crazy urge to bury her face in his shoulder and sob.

"I understand," he said. "Well, in that case, Natalie, I—"

He was interrupted by a knock on the door. A blonde woman who'd introduced herself to Natalie earlier as the church pianist poked her head in the room, her eyes wide. "There you are, Pastor Stone! I'm so sorry to interrupt, but there's a lady out here who *really* wants a word with you."

"Step aside, please." Natalie winced as she recognized the voice booming from the hallway. She really didn't feel up to coping with Adam's grandmother right now.

Cora Larkey pushed herself into the small room, the stiff veil on her lime-green hat trembling. Her entire outfit was the same shade, and she had the white rose corsage Natalie had given her earlier pinned to her substantial bosom.

"This wedding was supposed to start a half hour ago. What's going on?" Cora's blue eyes flittered between Natalie and the minister. "Where's my grandson? And who on earth are you?"

The last question was directed at Jacob Stone, who cast a quick, concerned glance at Natalie before rising from his seat. He introduced himself to the elderly lady and ushered her into the chair he'd just vacated.

Natalie wished he hadn't. As Cora sank down, a dense cloud of her expensive perfume replaced the light scent of his soap, making Natalie feel faintly queasy.

The minister unfolded a metal chair that had been leaning against one wall and sat down across from them. Natalie listened tensely as he repeated his news to Cora, adding some details that made Natalie cringe. Now she was the one bracing for an explosion. She knew from personal experience that Adam's grandmother didn't take bad news well.

"He did *what*?" Sure enough, Cora started spluttering in the middle of the explanation. "That *aggravating* boy! Of course," she added quickly, darting an alarmed look at the minister's face, "he's young. He'll come around and do the right thing eventually, I'm sure. But this is quite…difficult." Her small eyes flickered back over to Natalie. "Could I have a moment alone with the bride, Pastor? The two of us need to talk privately."

"Of course." The minister stood. Judging by that relieved look on his face, Adam wasn't the only man who wanted to run away from her today. "I'll be just outside if you need me."

As soon as he'd closed the door, the older woman shifted in her chair and pointed a finger at Natalie. "I should have known the two of you would pull something like this. Well, it won't work. I made myself very clear. You're not getting any help from me until you're decently married."

"I had nothing to do with this!"

"You expect me to believe that? You never wanted to have this wedding in a church. You made that very plain."

"I just thought a civil ceremony would be less stressful for everybody, and more appropriate, given the…circumstances. That's all."

"The Larkeys do not marry in courthouses. And the *circumstances* you find yourself in are your own fault."

"Not only mine."

Cora made an impatient noise. "Of course not. And that's why we're here. So that Adam can do the responsible thing for once in his life. I should never have left him alone. I should have been watching him like a hawk."

"But I never wanted to force Adam into this. If he really doesn't want to get married…" Natalie trailed off. She had no idea what to say next.

She'd truly believed that this wedding was God's answer to her prayers. When Cora had talked Adam into proposing, Natalie had set her own doubts aside, gathered up her fragile faith and put all her eggs in one shaky basket.

And now that basket had climbed out the church window and left her to deal with his grandmother.

Sometimes, Natalie reflected, life was just not fair.

"Don't be silly," Cora was saying. "Of course Adam doesn't want to get married, but what choice does he have now? You certainly can't take proper care of that baby on your own. You have no education, no job, no family worth talking about."

"I had a job up until last week. I only quit it because I was moving here."

"Waitressing at that tacky little diner? That hardly counts. And no great-grandchild of mine is going to be brought up in an Atlanta housing project, I'll tell you that."

Natalie pressed her lips together tightly and said nothing. There was nothing to say. On that one point, she and Cora were in total agreement.

"Adam has to go through with this marriage, for that innocent baby's sake," Cora continued. "Although goodness knows, I don't see what else *I* can do. That boy has hoodwinked me for the last time. I've already told him, unless he does the proper thing, he'll not see another cent from me. And believe you me, I meant it."

"I know you did." Adam had known it, too, which was why he'd suddenly resurfaced after months of dodging her phone calls and texts. It was humiliating to know that it took the prospect of losing his grandmother's money to get Adam to propose. But when you were buying your maternity clothes at thrift stores and could barely afford even the small co-pays for the local public health clinic, pride was a little out of your price range.

Even so, Natalie hadn't much liked the idea

of a shotgun wedding, but she'd wavered when Cora had discussed setting up a college fund for the baby. Then Cora had mentioned giving them her late husband's hobby farm to live on.

The promise of the farm had finally done it. Natalie had looked around her shabby apartment, awash with flashing lights from the police car parked outside her building for the third time that week. She'd imagined her son roaming the housing project with the other children of the overworked mothers, most of them single like her.

She'd known exactly where that path could lead. Just last week she'd tried to comfort a neighbor whose fourteen-year-old son had been arrested for selling drugs. The neighbor wasn't a bad mother. She just wasn't a match for the bad influences that lurked on every trash-littered corner of this neighborhood.

If Natalie stayed, one day her child could be the one in trouble. She couldn't let that happen, and she couldn't get out of there on her own.

Not soon enough, anyway.

Cora was right, Natalie had decided. The best thing to do was marry Adam and make it work somehow. Their baby was all that mattered.

"Oh well," Cora was saying irritably. "I expect I'll hear from Adam when he gets to the bottom of his bank account, and that shouldn't take long. That boy's never earned an honest dollar in his life, in spite of that pricey college degree I paid for." Cora's eyes skimmed Natalie's rounded figure. "Thankfully, the baby's not due for another three weeks, so a few more days shouldn't matter. You'll just have to stay put while we wait Adam out." The older woman pushed up from her seat and started for the door. Alarmed, Natalie struggled to her feet, as well.

Cora wanted her to wait here? In Pine Valley? How was she supposed to do that?

Cora already had her hand on the doorknob.

"I don't have any place to stay." Natalie's cheeks burned as she blurted out her admission. She'd given up her apartment, and she couldn't check back in to the ratty motel where she'd spent the last two nights. It might be the cheapest place in town, but it was still out of her price range.

Cora halted, frowning. "Well, you certainly can't come home with me. My retirement complex has very strict rules." She hesitated, then shrugged. "Fine. Here." She rummaged in the green purse swinging at her elbow and brought out an old-fashioned key. "I suppose you can go on out to Lark Hill. Adam's been staying there for the past week, supposedly making some repairs. You know how men are when they're living alone. I expect by now the house needs a good cleaning. You might as well spend your time doing that until he turns back up."

Lark Hill.

Even the name was beautiful. Natalie had been daydreaming about that farm for weeks. She felt a rush of sweet relief.

Thank You, God.

Maybe, just maybe, He hadn't completely abandoned her, after all.

"But mind you, this is a temporary arrangement. I won't sign over the deed until the two of you are married. And if I were you," Cora continued, "I'd stay out at Lark Hill and keep to myself as much as possible until all this is settled. People are a lot more old-fashioned in these small towns than they are in Atlanta. There's no sense stirring up any more gossip. Folks will have plenty to say about your…situation as it is. Oh, they'll be nice, at least to your face. Some of the churches may even offer to help you, but—"

"Don't worry. I won't need any help," Natalie interrupted. *Especially not from a church*, she finished silently. Cora's warning wasn't necessary. Atlanta wasn't as different from Pine Valley as Adam's grandmother seemed to think. "I'm used to taking care of myself."

"Good. Now—" Cora drew in a deep breath "—I'm going to go home. This whole thing has been *most* unpleasant. When Adam calls about the money, I'll let you know." With that, the older woman bustled out of the room, leaving the door ajar.

Money. Natalie's eyes widened as an awful realization hit her like a slap. She'd only brought her purse and a little overnight bag into the church. Nothing else. She'd left all the rest of her belongings in the back of Adam's Jeep. That meant Adam had driven off with everything she owned, including the small amount of money she'd hidden in her suitcase after cashing her last paycheck. It wasn't much, but apart from a couple of twenties tucked in her billfold, it was every penny she had in the world.

What was she going to do?

If Adam found that money, he'd spend it. Even if he didn't find it, Adam was awfully good at mooching. In spite of Cora's predictions, there was really no telling when he might show up. The baby wasn't due for nearly another month, but on her last clinic visit, she'd been told that he might come early. Any day now, the doctor had said.

Natalie suddenly found it hard to breathe, and the cramped dressing room began to spin.

"Miss Davis? Natalie! You need to sit down." A deep voice spoke urgently in front of her. She was dimly aware of a pressure on her arms, pushing her back into the chair. "Breathe. In and out. Good, slow breaths."

She followed his instructions. In and out. The swirling mist in her mind cleared, and she was able to focus her eyes on Pastor Jacob Stone's face.

He'd gone pale. "I'm calling 911."

"No! No, I'm all right," she managed. She didn't have the money to pay for an emergency room visit, or anything else.

He looked unconvinced. "In your condition, it might be a good idea to get checked out. You have to think about your baby."

Natalie's hand strayed to her rounded stomach. Ever since the ultrasound technician had told her she was having a boy, she'd been thinking about nothing *but* her baby. Right then and there, she'd made her child a silent promise.

You're not going to be like me. You're going to have a good life.

Remembering that moment now, she felt a fresh rush of resolve. She meant to keep that promise. Her son was going to grow up healthy and strong in a safe place, and he was going to finish high school and maybe even go to college.

"Natalie?"

Jacob Stone was still waiting for her answer. She took a steadying breath. "I'm fine, really. I'm just tired. It's been a hard day."

"I'd say that's an understatement." The sympathetic lines around his eyes deepened, and he gave her arm a gentle squeeze. "This is all going to work out, Natalie. I know it doesn't seem like it right now, but it will." He sounded so sure; she almost believed him. "In the meantime, is there anything I can do for you? Anything at all?"

Natalie tightened her fingers, pressing the hard metal key into her palm. Cora's blunt warning echoed in her memory. *They may offer to help you.*

But what choice did she have?

She cleared her throat. "As a matter of fact, there is…"

Chapter Two

"Could you give me a ride?" Natalie asked. "My car wouldn't start this morning. Adam had to drive to the motel to pick me up." Her poor old car had rattled all the way here from Atlanta, and she'd prayed every mile that it wouldn't strand her on the side of the road.

It hadn't, but it had sure been as dead as a rock this morning.

"Absolutely." The pastor spoke firmly. "I'll take you anyplace you want to go."

"Thank you." She offered him the brightest smile she could manage. It must not have been very convincing because that sympathy crinkled around his eyes again.

He gathered up her overnight case and tucked her Bible under his arm. "My truck is just outside."

Pastor Stone asked her to wait in the hallway

while he had a quick word with the group of people lingering in the sanctuary. Natalie kept her gaze on the floor, but she could feel their curious looks. She was glad when the minister came back and led the way out the big front doors of the church into the drizzly afternoon. To her surprise, he veered toward a battered blue pickup and opened the passenger side door.

This old beater didn't look much better than her car. It sure wasn't the kind of vehicle she'd expect a minister to drive, but it obediently rumbled to life when he twisted the key.

He shrugged off his suit jacket and held it out to her. "That dress looks thin. You've got to be cold, and it'll take the truck a few minutes to warm up. This weather is weird for April, isn't it? Usually we're all running our air conditioners by now, but this year winter just keeps hanging on."

She hesitated, but he was right. She was freezing. She took his jacket, tucking it over herself like a blanket. The warm satiny lining felt comforting against her chill-bumped arms, and it smelled like the soap she'd noticed earlier.

He raised his eyebrows. "So, where can I take you?"

"405 Chinaberry Road." She'd been reciting that address over and over to herself ever since

Cora had first told her about the farm. "Do you know where that is?"

"Sure." The minister leaned back in the seat of the rumbling truck, looking confused. "That's the old Lark Hill farm. Why do you want to go out there?"

"Adam's grandmother is letting me stay there until…for the time being." He was frowning, and she felt a warning tickle along her arms that had nothing to do with the cold. "What's wrong?"

"Nothing, just…has Mrs. Larkey seen the place lately?"

"I'm not sure, but she said Adam's been staying there for the past week. Why?"

"Nobody's lived at Lark Hill in the five years I've been in Pine Valley. Last time I drove by, it was looking pretty run-down. In your condition…" He hesitated.

Was that all? That was nothing. She'd stayed in plenty of places that made *run-down* look good. "Don't worry about me. I'm not a very fancy person, Pastor Stone."

He hesitated a second, then shrugged. "I guess we can at least go take a look." He shifted the truck into gear and headed out of the parking lot. "And you can call me Jacob. Everybody does." He offered her a sideways glance and a smile. "I'm not a very fancy person, either."

Natalie nodded and adjusted the seat belt across her baby bump. Riding in a car was so uncomfortable these days. Then again, everything was.

The preacher shot her an apologetic look. "It's going to be about a ten-minute drive. Lark Hill's kind of out in the middle of nowhere."

The middle of nowhere. In spite of everything, Natalie's lips curved into a smile. She'd lived in overcrowded housing projects all her life.

The middle of nowhere sounded wonderful.

Adam just *had* to show up and go through with their wedding. Cora had made herself very clear. No marriage, no farm.

No future.

Natalie turned her face toward the window and squeezed her eyes shut. *Please, Lord. You know I can't provide a good life for this baby all by myself. Please, let Adam come back.*

A few minutes later, Jacob slowed and put on his turn signal, although as far as Natalie could see, there wasn't another car for miles.

"Here we are," he said. A tilted sign announced Lark Hill Farm in weather-beaten blue paint. The faded silhouette of a bird perched on the bar of the *H*, its beak lifted in a silent song.

Natalie winced as the pickup bumped over the ruts of the overgrown driveway, but she forgot her physical misery when she caught her first glimpse of the farmhouse. Her heart sped up as she gazed at the view through the smudged windshield.

This place was just perfect.

This place was just awful.

Jacob slowed the truck to a gentle stop, but he didn't bother to turn off the engine. There was no way they'd be staying here for very long. He'd been polite when he'd described the old farm as run-down.

It was a dump.

The tiny one-story farmhouse was covered in peeling white paint. A couple of scraggly chickens were scratching in the dead leaves littering its sagging porch. Beyond the house was a gray rough-lumber barn that had half collapsed. A makeshift fence had been attached to the part that was still standing, and an animal with a multicolored coat and large curved horns peered curiously through the rusty wires.

Natalie pointed. "What's that?"

Jacob's heart sank to his toes, along with his general opinion of humanity. "That's Rufus. What's he doing here?"

"What's a Rufus?"

"The most troublesome billy goat in four counties." Jacob shook his head. "No telling who stuck Adam with him. That animal's been passed around more than the common cold. Nobody keeps him for long."

Natalie leaned forward in her seat, peering through the window. "The poor thing. He doesn't look mean."

"He's not. He's just…irritating. And there's not a fence made that can hold him."

He heard a click and turned to see that Natalie had shrugged off his coat and was unsnapping her seat belt.

"Whoa." Without thinking, he leaned over and caught her hand as she reached for the door lever. It felt small and chilly in his. "What are you doing?"

She stared at him. "I'm going to look around."

Jacob hesitated, but she seemed pretty determined. "All right. But wait there. I'll come around and walk with you. There's junk all over this yard, and you don't want to fall."

She already had her door open, but she stopped, looking surprised. "Oh! Okay. Thank you."

He came around and helped her out of the truck. "Take my arm." Without waiting for her answer, he took her right hand in his and placed his other arm around her waist. In spite of her pregnancy, she felt as fragile as a bird. They walked slowly toward the house, the hem of her light dress fluttering in the fitful breeze.

When they reached the porch, he halted. "These steps look pretty rickety." He tested the bottom one. It groaned but didn't break.

"They seem fine." She started to move forward, but he stopped her gently.

"Let me go first." He definitely didn't need a pregnant lady crashing through some rotten board. He edged in front of her, bouncing on the remaining steps before allowing Natalie to put her weight on them. The old boards protested, but they held together.

As he led her through the leaves toward the front door, he heard a quiet sniffle. He glanced back to catch Natalie swiping a tear off her cheek.

He'd been expecting this ever since he'd told her about Adam.

"Are you okay?" He regretted his choice of words the minute they were out of his mouth. Stupid question. Of course she wasn't okay.

She shook her head and managed a wobbly smile. "Don't pay any attention to me. I'm fine. Really. It's just…"

As he watched her struggle for words, his heart swelled with sympathy. First the wedding disappointment and now this disaster of a house. He waited, praying for the ability to help her cope with whatever feelings she managed to get out. "It's okay, Natalie. Go ahead and say whatever you need to say. Yell if you want to. After the day you've had, I wouldn't blame you a bit."

"No, it's not that." She sputtered a teary little laugh and dabbed at her eyes again. "It's just… you're being so *nice* to me, holding my arm and walking me up on the porch and all. Don't mind me. I cry about all sorts of stupid stuff these days. Hormones, I guess." She gave him a trembling smile. "Wait just a minute. I put the house key in my purse."

Jacob didn't smile back. He stood silently on the sagging porch, watching the wind tease strands of Natalie's hair loose as she searched for the key.

He was usually pretty quick with words, but right now, he couldn't think of a single thing to say. After all Natalie had been through today, *that* was what finally made her cry? The fact that he wouldn't let a pregnant woman walk on a half-rotten porch without checking it first?

What kind of life had this woman led?

I don't have much family. When Natalie had made that quiet admission back at the church, he'd felt a surge of compassion so strong that it had surprised him. He'd always been a sucker for people in trouble, but he hadn't wanted to help somebody this badly in a long, long time.

He didn't have much family either, and he knew firsthand how tough that could be. But, of course, loneliness wasn't the only thing he and Natalie Davis had in common.

Not by a long shot.

The instant he'd caught sight of Natalie's pregnant profile, he'd known. None of this was accidental. It couldn't be. Of all the ministers in the surrounding area, as far as he knew, he was the only one who knew firsthand what it was like to struggle with an out-of-wedlock pregnancy.

This situation had God's fingerprints all over it.

The mistakes Jacob had made before he'd become a Christian still broke his heart, and there wasn't a thing he could do about them. But he could certainly do something about this.

"I'm going to help you." He didn't realize he'd spoken aloud until she answered him.

"Well, okay. Thanks." She handed him a long metal key. "It looks really old. I hope it works."

She thought he meant help with the antique lock. He accepted the key automatically and turned to the door, glad to have something to do until he could think straight again.

The lock was tarnished and flecked with decades of old paint, but the key turned easily enough. He pushed the door open, and a puff of musty air brushed their faces.

The door opened into a small rectangular living room. Dust flurried in the weak sunlight coming through the generous windows, and furry gray cobwebs dangled from the bead board ceiling.

The room looked like it had been furnished by somebody's maiden aunt. There was a beige camelback sofa and two drab olive armchairs, all sporting fussy lace circlets on their arms and backs. A couple of spindly legged tables laden with dusty knickknacks were angled in the corners.

"Oh my," Natalie breathed beside him, poking her head in to get a better view. He glanced down and was surprised by the rapt expression on her face. He'd expected a wrinkled nose, but she didn't seem put off at all.

He frowned and took a second look at the room. Maybe it did have a certain appeal to it.

If you didn't have a dust allergy.

Natalie edged past him into the house and touched one of the lace doilies with a gentle finger. "It's like stepping back in time, isn't it?" She opened a nearby door and disappeared into the adjoining room.

"Watch your step, now." Jacob warned as he

followed her. He hoped the rest of this place was sturdier than that porch.

The house was tiny, so their tour didn't take long. They passed through two small bedrooms furnished with iron beds and discovered a bathroom complete with a stained claw-foot tub. When Natalie paused to twist a faucet on the pedestal sink, a stream of clear water ran into the grubby basin. She glanced up at him, smiling.

"This water doesn't smell all chemically like the water back in Atlanta."

"This far out of town, it would have to be well water. No chlorine." He hadn't seen Natalie Davis really smile until now. He'd thought she was a nice-looking woman before, but with that happy expression on her face, she was downright beautiful.

The smile lingered on her lips as she pushed open the last door. It led them into the kitchen.

Natalie halted on the threshold. "Oh!"

Jacob took in the sight in front of them, and his lips tightened. No wonder she didn't want to go any farther. The other rooms hadn't been very clean, but this one took dirty to a whole new level.

Once upon a time, somebody had painted the kitchen walls a light yellow, but the cheery paint was filmed over with a thick layer of dust.

Dingy white curtains embroidered with trios of red cherries hung limply at the windows. A small red-and-white enameled table, its surface covered with food wrappers, sat in the middle of a scabby linoleum floor. A generous double-basined sink was positioned underneath the window, flanked by old-fashioned metal cabinets. A boxy gas stove with two ovens hunkered in one corner, and an elderly refrigerator chugged next to it.

Every available surface was littered with trash. If Adam Larkey had gone through with his wedding, *this* was what he'd have brought his pregnant bride home to? After what had happened back at the church, Jacob hadn't thought his opinion of the guy could drop much lower.

He'd been wrong.

"I think we've seen enough," he said quietly. "I'll drive you back to town."

Natalie didn't answer. She was standing with her eyes closed, her whole body tensed. One hand was clutching the door frame, clenching down so hard that her knuckles were white.

"Natalie?" He wasn't sure what was happening, but from the look on her face, it couldn't be good.

"Contraction," she whispered.

Chapter Three

Finally the cramp ebbed away. Natalie relaxed and opened her eyes. Jacob was watching her, his face tight with concern.

"I'm okay," she said quickly. "That was just a Braxton Hicks. I've been having them for a while now. The doctor says they're perfectly normal." She managed a shaky smile. Normal, yes. Fun, not so much.

"Whew." Relief washed over his face. "I thought it was the real thing there for a minute."

"Not time for that yet." She spoke lightly, but she remembered another thing the obstetrician had said on her last visit to the clinic. *First babies don't pay much attention to their due dates.*

She sure hoped her baby would be the exception because she wasn't even close to being ready. All her plans were falling apart. She had no husband, no money. She didn't even have a crib, and all the secondhand baby clothes she'd bought had driven away with Adam in the back of his Jeep.

Natalie straightened her shoulders. There was no point wasting time feeling sorry for herself. She had more important things to do right now. She needed to sit down and start figuring out how she could manage on her own until Adam showed back up.

If he showed up.

"Thanks for driving me out here, Jacob. I don't want to take up any more of your time, so I'll let you get on back to town." She tilted up her chin and tried a smile. "And anyway, it looks like I have a little cleaning to do."

"No." Jacob was shaking his head before she'd even finished speaking. "I'm not leaving you out here alone. Not in your condition." He scanned the messy room, his face tight with disgust. "And you definitely shouldn't be cleaning up a disaster like this."

In spite of the day she'd had, Natalie nearly laughed out loud. There was nothing wrong here that some soapy water and a few big trash bags couldn't fix. Jacob might have had a lot more schooling than she'd had, but right now he didn't have a clue what he was talking about.

She'd cleaned up messes way worse than this. "I'm not afraid of a little dirt."

"This is more than a little dirt. Look, let me give you a ride back to town. We'll find you another place to stay. If money's an issue, I can give my church a call—"

Cora's warning replayed itself in Natalie's memory, and she cut him off firmly. "I appreciate that, but I'm staying here. Adam's grandma is sure he'll be back by tomorrow or the next day."

Jacob looked around the room again and started rolling up the sleeves of his dress shirt. "Then I'll help you clean this up."

Natalie felt a stir of panic. "No need for that. I've worked as a waitress ever since I…got out of school. Believe me, I can clean up a kitchen without any help." She'd almost said *dropped out*, but she'd caught herself just in time. She didn't want to admit to this man that she'd quit school when she was sixteen. It was a choice she'd always regretted, but at the time it had seemed like the only way to get out of her mother's apartment—and away from her mom's endless parade of hard-partying boyfriends.

A little over a year ago, she'd gathered up her courage and enrolled in free GED classes at a nearby community center. To her relief, she'd managed the classwork pretty well, and she'd passed the test with flying colors. She'd daydreamed about taking some college night courses, maybe even becoming a teacher one day. She loved the idea of teaching children.

Of course, when two blue lines had shown up on her pregnancy test, all those plans had come to a screeching halt. Dreams like that were for women who didn't have babies to take care of.

Jacob was looking at her with a concerned crease between his eyebrows. "I can't leave you here to deal with this all by yourself."

"That's sweet, but I'd really rather you did. I want to be alone for a while. I have a lot to think about, and cleaning is like therapy for me." Maybe that was stretching the truth a little, but she was starting to feel desperate.

Pastor Jacob Stone was a very hard man to shoo away.

Jacob was silent for a moment, studying her. She kept her eyes on his and waited him out.

It worked. Although he clearly wasn't happy, after a minute he blew out a slow breath and shrugged. "Well. If you're sure that's what you really want..."

"It is."

To her horror, he pulled out a worn leather wallet. "Here. At least let me—" he started.

"I don't *need* your money." She flushed at the startled expression on his face. Maybe she had been a little too forceful, but she didn't want this minister's charity. She'd already been humiliated enough for one day. "Thank you, though," she added belatedly. He'd gone out of his way to be kind. She could at least be polite.

"I was going to give you a card with my cell number on it." He pulled one out and held it in her direction. Pine Valley Community Church was written in blocky blue letters across the top of it. "I want you to promise to call me if you need anything. Okay? Anything at all."

"Thank you." She wouldn't call, of course. She didn't need this man or his church involved in her problems. She'd find a way to deal with them herself, like she always had.

Granted, she'd never had problems quite this big before. But she'd manage.

Somehow.

"I'll bring in your overnight bag before I leave. And I'll be back to check on you tomorrow after services."

Natalie shook her head. She was having enough trouble getting him to leave this time. She didn't need to go through all this again tomorrow. "You don't have to do that. I'll be fine."

His mouth hardened into a stubborn line. "You're stranded out here without a car. I don't even like leaving you overnight. Are you *sure* I can't talk you into going back to town?"

"Yes." She spoke firmly, but softened her refusal with a smile. "Completely sure."

"Then I'll see you around lunchtime. No," he interjected as she opened her mouth to argue again. "It's not up for debate. I'm coming back. I'm a minister, remember, and helping people through difficult situations is what I do. I'm here for the duration, Natalie. Until we get your situation more…stable, you can consider me your right-hand guy. Okay?"

It wasn't the least bit okay, but how could she explain that? He was smiling at her, a friendly smile that came complete with a set of boyish dimples. But underneath all that charm, she saw a firmness that made her heart sink right down to the toes she hadn't seen for the last month and a half.

Natalie had dealt with enough bullheaded people in her life to recognize stubbornness when she saw it. Jacob Stone wasn't going to budge, so she might as well give in now as later.

"Suit yourself. But it really isn't necessary."

She didn't sound particularly gracious, but he didn't seem to mind. "I'll see you tomorrow, then." Casting one last uneasy look around the cluttered room, he headed for the door.

When the rumbles of his truck finally faded into the distance, Natalie sank onto a sticky chair and rubbed her chilled arms.

Alone for the first time since she'd heard the news about Adam, she realized how comforting Jacob's company had been. Even if he *was* a minister, he was also a friendly, concerned human being. Without him, the house felt colder and dirtier, and the reality of how alone she truly was began to seep in.

She would *not* cry, pregnancy hormones or not. She was a Christian now, wasn't she? All those encouraging devotionals she'd been reading told her to pray and trust God when things went wrong. Granted, right now that seemed nearly impossible, but what choice did she have? She shut her eyes and clasped her hands together.

Lord, this sure isn't the way I thought today would turn out. I read in the Bible that Your strength is made perfect in weakness. I hope You meant that because I'm just about as weak as anybody can get right now. Please...help me.

She opened her eyes, but the scene in front of her hadn't changed. Her gaze wandered over the room, lingering on the litter of food wrappers and the pile of dirty dishes in the sink. She glanced down at her left hand, still bare, resting on a pregnant tummy that seemed to get bigger by the minute.

None of that was too encouraging.

Her cell phone suddenly erupted in a burst of reggae music, and she gasped, digging wildly in her purse. That was Adam's ringtone. Her hands were shaking so hard that it took her three tries to answer the call.

"Adam?"

There was a silence on the other end of the line, then a sheepish sigh. "Sorry, Nat. I kind of freaked out."

He sounded like a guilty kid, and she'd never liked the nickname Nat. Still, getting angry with Adam never helped. Natalie rubbed her temples wearily. "Where are you?"

"I'm crashing at Gary's place for a few days."

Natalie frowned. "You drove all the way to Tennessee?"

"I didn't know where else to go. I just snapped."

Natalie's head was beginning to pound, and she was feeling a little shaky. She'd been too nervous to eat breakfast or lunch today. "You snapped."

"Well, yeah. The last couple of days out on the farm, I kept remembering how Grampa Ed loved that old place. He always talked about retiring there and growing blueberries, but Nana Cora wouldn't let him. She wanted to stay in Fairmont. That's all I could think about today at the church, you know? How Grampa Ed never got to do anything he wanted, and how I'm going to be just like him."

She couldn't muster up too much sympathy for Adam, or his grampa Ed either, for that matter. But of course, Adam had a right to make his own choices, no matter what his grandmother thought.

"Adam, look. If you really don't want to get married…"

"Come on, Nat. Let's be honest. Neither one of us really wants to get married, but we're stuck because of this baby thing."

She started to argue but stopped. It was the truth.

She didn't really want to marry Adam. She just wanted a better life for her baby than she could provide on her own. And Adam wanted to hang on to his grandmother's good graces, and more importantly, her checking account.

What a mess they'd made.

"So what are we going to do?"

"Get married, I guess. What choice do we have?"

"So you're coming back?"

"Yeah. But—"

"But what?"

She heard Adam take a breath, then the words tumbled out. "Here's the thing, Nat. Gary and some buds of his are leaving tomorrow to hike a leg of the Appalachian Trail, and I want to go with them."

What? Whatever she'd expected Adam to say,

it hadn't been that. "You want to hike the Appalachian Trail? *Now?*"

"Just part of it. It'll only take about two weeks, and I think it'll help clear my head, you know? I've already talked to Nana Cora, and she's good with it because we'll still have enough time to get married before the baby comes."

"That's cutting it kind of close, Adam." The doctor's warning sounded in her mind.

Any day now.

"It's only for a couple of weeks, Nat. And then I'll have to be boring and responsible for the rest of my life."

Natalie felt a twinge of guilt. There sure wasn't much left now of the carefree confidence that had attracted her to Adam in the first place.

She remembered the first time he'd walked into the diner. She'd been working the second leg of an exhausting double shift, and Adam had blown in like a refreshing breeze. He was just coming back from a white-water rafting trip, and he'd had a tattered backpack slung over one shoulder and a gigantic grin on his face. To Natalie's tired eyes, he'd looked like freedom, romance and adventure all rolled up into one slightly rumpled guy. When he'd asked for her number, she'd broken her long-standing policy and written it down on a napkin.

Back then, she hadn't had her faith to steady

her, and she'd fallen for Adam too hard and too fast, blindly assuming that his feelings were keeping pace with hers. The situation they were in now was every bit as much her fault as his.

"All right," she heard herself agreeing. "Two weeks."

"Awesome." A hint of the joy she remembered was in the word. "Nana Cora said you were going to wait on the farm. I left some food in the kitchen. Oh! I…uh…meant to clean that up, by the way. And there's a goat out back. Some guy gave him to me for free, along with four bags of chow. He even threw in a few chickens… Look, Gary's calling me. We're planning to hit the trail first thing in the morning, so I've got to go. See you in two weeks, Nat."

"Adam—" Natalie began, but he'd already hung up.

She sat there, holding the silent phone in her hand. So that was that. She was officially on her own for the next two weeks.

The baby shifted position, reminding her that she wasn't really on her own anymore. She had somebody else to take care of now.

Which reminded her, she needed to eat something.

She went to inspect the contents of the refrigerator and the kitchen cupboards. The food Adam had mentioned seemed to be mostly po-

tato chips and cheese puffs, but she finally managed to locate a fairly fresh loaf of bread and a
half-empty jar of peanut butter.

The idea of eating in the dirty kitchen wasn't
very appealing, so she decided to take her sandwich outside. She could eat it while she checked
out the rest of the farm.

She hadn't realized how musty the house
smelled until she stepped out the door into the
fresh air. A brisk wind was blowing the last of
the gray clouds away, and the sky arching over
the farmyard was a sweet eggshell blue.

As she picked her way carefully through the
overgrown grass, she startled five striped chickens, who squawked and flapped away. When
she reached the barn, the shaggy goat with the
patchy brown-and-black fur trotted up to his
fence and bleated at her.

She stuck out a hesitant finger to stroke his
satiny nose. He tipped up a bearded chin and
nibbled lightly on her thumb before bleating
again. Natalie peered into his pen. His water
trough was half-full, but a battered tin pan sat
empty by the fence.

"Are you hungry?" The goat made his sad
noise again, so she offered him the last bite of
her sandwich. He gobbled it up and looked at
her expectantly.

He *was* hungry. Adam had mentioned some

feed. Maybe it was in the barn. She pulled open the rough door and looked in. The building had a dirt floor and smelled damp. Natalie shuddered.

There was a second half-opened door to her right, and she thought she could see some yellow bags stacked inside a small room. She took a step in that direction.

Something scrabbled in the depths of the closet-like space, and she froze.

Please, Lord, don't let that be a rat. I can't handle a rat right now, not after the day I've had. I just can't.

The goat cried out again, and she bit her lip. The poor thing was starving. Rat or not, she was going to have to get to that feed. Gathering her courage, she crossed the dirt floor and pulled the door to the room fully open.

Something flew up toward her face in a flurry of feathers and dust. She cried out and jumped backward, stumbling over a couple of rusty paint cans. She caught herself against a wooden post just before she fell, and she heard her dress rip as the fabric snagged on a protruding nail.

The escaping hen clucked loudly as it scurried out into the sunshine. Natalie stayed where she was, breathing hard and waiting for her hammering heart to slow down.

She was all right. It was just a chicken. She hadn't fallen. The baby was fine.

"Bleaaah!"

The loud noise sounded right beside her, and she yelped in alarm. Rufus was standing in the cobweb-filled barn, looking at her with his weird golden eyes. How had he gotten out of his pen so fast?

"Bleaaah," he bleated at her again.

"Shoo, Rufus. Go away!" The goat just tilted his head and watched her.

If she had some feed, she might be able to lure him back into his pen, but she really didn't want to go into that spooky room. No telling what else was hiding in there. The chicken sure had been in a hurry to get out.

The feelings she'd been fighting off for hours swelled over her like a tidal wave. She was tired, her back hurt and she'd just ripped a hole in the only nice maternity dress she owned.

She was cornered in a spidery barn with a goat and scary chickens, and somehow she had to figure out how to take care of herself and these animals for the next two weeks on the forty dollars she had in her purse. And if the baby came early, she'd have to take care of him, too.

All by herself.

There was no way she could do this.

Natalie felt the sobs start from somewhere deep down, and this time she didn't have enough strength to stop them. She leaned against the splintery post and cried her heart out while Rufus nibbled on the hem of her ruined dress.

The midday sun streamed through the stained glass windows of the Pine Valley Community Church sanctuary as the pianist began the last verse of the morning's closing hymn. Jacob sang along with his congregation, profoundly relieved to see the worship hour come to a close.

He was anxious to get out to Lark Hill and check on Natalie Davis.

He'd spent a restless night imagining every kind of disaster that could possibly happen to a pregnant woman out at the old Larkey farm. It had turned out to be an impressive list. He never should have left Natalie out there alone, no matter what she said.

After pronouncing the benediction, he posted himself in his usual spot at the church entryway, prepared to offer handshakes and hugs as his church family filed past him. Today the line moved a lot more quickly than it usually did. Nobody seemed to want to linger and chat, and normally friendly people were having a hard time meeting his eyes. In fact, he noticed that several members slipped out the side door without speaking to him at all.

Something was definitely up with his little flock. But what?

He hadn't had a chance to check in with Arlene before the service, so he'd have to wait to find out. Arlene would know what was going on. She always did.

The arrival of four-year-old Katie Barker was a welcome distraction. Completely unaffected by the tension around her, she threw her arms around his neck and kissed his cheek as soon as he crouched down within her range.

"This is for you, Pastor," she announced, handing him a dampish mound of green clay with various lumps sticking out if it. "I made it in Sunday school. It's the turtle from Noah's ark."

"I can see that," Jacob fibbed with a smile. "Wow. And you made it for me?"

"No, I made it for my daddy, but one of its legs fell off and Tommy Anderson stepped on it and smushed it before I could stick it back on. I'm going to make Daddy a better turtle, and you can have this one. Because you're nobody's daddy, and a three-legged turtle is better than no turtle at all."

The few church members still within earshot chuckled, and Katie's mother flushed bright pink. Jacob offered the flustered woman a reassuring smile before turning his attention back to the little girl.

"That's true, Katie-bug. I don't have anybody to make me turtles, so I'm extra glad to have this one. I'll put it in my office so I can see it every day." He'd add it to the collection of Vacation Bible School crafts and Sunday school projects that Arlene was always pestering him to throw away.

His secretary was wasting her breath because he planned to hang on to every lopsided Popsicle stick and faded scrap of construction paper on that shelf. Katie Barker had summed up why with the artless truthfulness of a preschooler. Three-legged turtles were better than no turtles at all.

Arlene, as usual, had stationed herself at the tail end of the line. She didn't bother to comment on his sermon. She never did. "When you preach a bad one, I'll let you know," she'd told him once.

He believed her.

"That piano needs tuning," his secretary informed him, riffling through her black purse for her car keys. "I'll set it up tomorrow morning." She scanned Jacob's face with narrowed eyes. "You don't look so well. I sure hope you haven't caught that flu Good Shepherd's passing around." She snorted. "Isn't that just like those folks? You go do them a favor, and what do they give you in return? Germs!"

Jacob rolled his eyes. Pine Valley Community and Good Shepherd had a long-standing, mostly amicable rivalry that had started on the softball field and which Arlene tended to take a little too seriously. And she wasn't the only one in his congregation who felt that way. Maybe it was time for him to give his We're All on the Same Team sermon.

Again.

"I'm fine, Arlene. Just tired. Listen, how much money do we have in our benevolence fund right now?"

"I don't know exactly." The concern in Arlene's expression shifted to suspicion. "I'd have to check. Jacob, this doesn't have anything to do with what happened at that wedding yesterday, does it? Because that poor bride is Good Shepherd's problem, not ours."

"I don't think she's a member there, and anyway, I was the minister present when everything went to pieces. I feel responsible for her."

"Well, you shouldn't." His secretary glanced warily in the direction of the door. She waited until the last members of the congregation were safely out of earshot before speaking again. "And I'll tell you this—after missing that meeting yesterday, the very *last* thing you need to do is start doling out our benevolence money to somebody who isn't even a member of our church."

"Was Digby that upset?"

"He wasn't upset at all, which was far worse, I can assure you. He spent the entire meeting hounding the church board about that fellowship hall. He's won over three more of the members. You know what that means."

Jacob's heart sank. He knew, all right. If it came to the floor now, the fellowship hall approval was only one vote shy of going through.

"And that's not the half of it. Digby brought up that nephew of his at least four times. He's graduated from seminary now, and what's worse, he's gotten married! Digby was passing the wedding photos all around the conference table."

Jacob started to chuckle, but he caught a glimpse of Arlene's expression and cleared his throat instead. He'd never seen her this upset before, not even on that Wednesday evening last summer when a bat had blundered into the sanctuary and started dive-bombing the senior ladies' prayer meeting.

"What's wrong with the nephew's wife?"

"Nothing! That's the problem. She's everything a minister's wife should be. The girl's a pianist, and her parents are missionaries. I'm telling you, it could hardly be any worse." His secretary glared at him suspiciously. "This isn't the *least bit* funny, Jacob. It was plain as day that Digby's angling to put his nephew in your place, and if you don't stop worrying about other churches' jilted brides and focus on your own problems, you may very well find yourself looking for another job!"

Chapter Four

Thanks to Arlene, it was nearly one thirty when Jacob finally drove up Lark Hill's rutted driveway. No battered Jeep was in sight, so the runaway groom must not have returned. Natalie was nowhere to be seen, either. She was probably inside resting with her feet up, or doing whatever else pregnant women were supposed to do, he told himself. That was most likely why the place looked so empty.

Still, he quickened his step as he mounted the shaky porch. He knocked firmly. "Natalie? It's Jacob Stone."

He had to knock twice before he heard her coming down the hall. When she finally opened the door, his heart lifted with sweet relief.

Natalie Davis was just fine.

She looked good, actually. Her brown hair was swept away from her face in a simple ponytail, and she was dressed in a blue-and-white-striped maternity top with matching pants. She'd folded the sleeves back over her elbows, and she clutched a damp rag in one hand. Even though the April afternoon was unseasonably chilly, there was a faint sheen of perspiration on her face, and she smelled like freshly sliced lemons.

She didn't, however, look very happy to see him. "Hi." The polite smile she offered him didn't quite reach her eyes.

He gave her his warmest one in return and hoped for the best. "Hi! I'm glad to see you survived the night." He made the comment lightly, but he meant every word of it. He wasn't about to leave Natalie out here alone again, not without setting some sensible safeguards in place.

Which was going to be difficult if he couldn't even make it past the door. "Do you have time for a quick visit?"

She bit her lip. "I'm…kind of busy right now. I'm cleaning."

Nice try, but during his time as a minister, Jacob had charmed his way past more doors than he could count. "Really? I'd love to see how the place is shaping up. I won't get in your way." He smiled again. "Scout's honor."

Natalie hesitated another few seconds. Then she sighed and opened the door. "All right." She poked her head out onto the porch and scanned the yard. "You'd better come in quick, though. That Rufus goat was out of his pen this morning, and he seems to want to come in the house. He was at the back door just a minute ago, but he can be really fast when he wants to be."

So could Jacob. He was inside before Natalie could change her mind.

Things at Lark Hill had definitely improved. The living room had been dusted, and an aqua-and-silver vacuum cleaner, the kind with a long hose attached to a round wheeled tub, sat in the middle of the floor. It looked ancient, but it must have worked because everything was a lot cleaner. She'd taken down the dingy curtains, and sunlight sparkled through the bare windows, casting golden rectangles on the floorboards.

"You really *have* been cleaning." It came out like an accusation. "Are you sure that's a good idea?"

She glanced up at him, her eyes startled wide. They were clear and bright today, and just the color of the spicy amber tea his grandmother had always brewed at Christmastime.

"I don't like dirt," she answered simply, "and anyway, I'm just using plain old dish soap and water. That's not going to hurt anything."

As Natalie led the way into the kitchen, Jacob halted in the doorway, stunned.

The litter of trash had vanished. The worn countertops and appliances shone, and the chipped enamel sink was empty of dishes. A raggedy broom leaned against one corner, the peeling linoleum floor was neatly swept and a bowl of sudsy water sat on the table. The lemony scent was strong in here. She must have been in the middle of scrubbing when he knocked.

This kitchen had been a complete disaster yesterday, but now it felt homier than his own bachelor apartment. Jacob shook his head slowly.

Women were amazing creatures.

But still… "I really don't think you should be working this hard."

She laughed, but there wasn't much humor in the sound. "Don't worry about me. I'm used to hard work." She pulled out one of the chairs and lowered herself into it slowly.

He dragged out a second chair and joined her at the table. "I'm guessing Adam didn't come back."

"No, but he called." Avoiding his eyes, Natalie dipped the rag into the bowl, wrung it out and busied herself scrubbing at a spot on the table. "He's coming back in two weeks. I'm going to stay here in the meantime and get things ready."

So the wedding was still on. Supposedly. But in Jacob's opinion, the rest of that plan was definitely a nonstarter. "You can't stay way out here on your own for that long in your condition. You don't even have a working car."

For a second or two, her rag stilled. Then she tightened her lips and began scrubbing even harder. "I'll be fine."

Jacob considered the stubborn set of Natalie's jaw with a sinking feeling. From the look of things, unless he was prepared to manhandle an extremely pregnant woman out of this house and into his truck, there wasn't much he could do.

But he had to do something.

He pulled out his cell phone and scrolled through his contacts until he found the one he was looking for. Two rings later, his call was answered.

"Hey, Mike. Listen, I need a favor. There's a car parked over by the Sunset Motel on Highway 36. Do you think you could tow it back to your garage and get it running?"

"What are you doing?" Natalie had straightened up in her chair, the dripping rag forgotten in her hand. She shook her head at him furiously, her ponytail swinging.

He held up one hand in a calming gesture. "Yeah, I know, Mike. You're always backed up, but this is an emergency. Like I said, I'm calling in that favor you owe me. Sure, tomorrow's fine. Yes, whatever it takes. Just fix it. I'll drop the keys off first thing in the morning." He ended the call and smiled at Natalie, who was staring at him with her mouth open. "Give me your keys, and I'll run them by Mike's garage tomorrow. He's a member of my church and the best mechanic in town. If anybody can get your car running, Mike can."

"I…" Natalie blinked at him. "I appreciate the thought, but you should have checked with me first. I'm on a…limited budget right now. I'd love to get an estimate, but I can't give the go-ahead for the repairs until I'm sure I can afford them."

"There's no way you can stay out here without a car. It's not safe. Don't worry about the cost. My church can help." They could. But would they? Given everything that was going on right now, he wasn't sure.

Well, it didn't matter. If the board wouldn't allow the benevolence fund to cover the repairs, Jacob would pay for them himself. Somehow.

"No!" The force of her refusal seemed to surprise her as much as it did him. She blushed and continued in a calmer voice. "It's really kind of you to offer, Jacob, but that wouldn't be right. I'm not even a member of your church."

"That's not a problem." It wasn't. Well, not to Jacob. "In any case, there's no point worrying about it until Mike gets back to us about the repairs. We don't even know what's wrong with your car yet. It might be an easy fix."

"I suppose." Although Natalie's expression made it clear that she doubted it.

"So. Now that we've got that settled, what else can I help you with today?"

Natalie hesitated. She wasn't sure what to do, and right now she didn't like any of her options very much.

She hated the thought of getting any more mixed up with Jacob Stone or that church he kept mentioning. But just before he'd arrived, she'd asked the Lord to help her manage until Adam came back. She couldn't afford to turn her nose up at His answer, just because it wasn't what she'd hoped for. And, she *was* stuck out here in the middle of nowhere without a vehicle and with nothing to eat but Adam's leftover junk food. If it wasn't for the baby, she'd make do, but…

Once again, there was no real choice to make.

"Do you have time to drive me to the supermarket? I can be ready to go really fast. I just need to do a quick check and see what I need." Probably everything, but given her lack of funds, she'd make sure.

"Sure," Jacob agreed instantly. "Take your time. While you make your list, I'll go put Rufus back in his pen for you and make a couple of phone calls."

Fifteen minutes later, they were rumbling toward town in Jacob's old truck. As he drove past fields dotted with grazing cows or rows of seedlings, Jacob kept up a friendly conversation about their various owners. Natalie nodded, but she wasn't really listening.

She went over and over her grocery list in her head, trying to decide which items were absolute necessities and which she could find a way to do without. She had to stretch her tiny amount of cash as far as she could.

In spite of her worries, she perked up when they reached the city limits sign, craning her neck as she peered through the smudged windshield. She'd fallen in love with the town of Pine Valley the minute she'd seen it.

This place had such a peaceful, unrushed air about it. And it was so pretty, too. A rosy brick courthouse sat proudly in the middle of a grassy square, ringed by old-fashioned stores advertising various kinds of businesses: a barbershop, a hardware store and a bookstore. Most of them had Sorry, We're Closed signs in their windows.

People in Pine Valley apparently took their Sunday rest seriously.

She expected Jacob to drive past the square, figuring there was probably a chain supermarket on the outskirts of town. Instead, he parked in front of a small storefront with bright green-and-white-striped awnings over its windows. Bailey's was written in flowing white script across the sparkling glass of the door. Through the wide windows, Natalie saw baskets of produce, invitingly angled to show off the vegetables and fruits to potential customers.

This was no supermarket. This was some sort of fancy food boutique that looked as if it might have a surcharge for just walking in the door. No way could she afford to shop in a place like this.

"Here we are." Jacob pulled his keys from the ignition. "You'll love this store. Bailey's always has the best stuff in town."

Maybe, but she didn't need the best stuff in town. She needed the cheapest stuff in town. Before she could figure out the least humiliating way to explain that, Jacob had rounded the truck and was opening the passenger side door.

"I only need a few things," she said quickly, "so this won't take long."

"I'm in no hurry. Here now, watch that curb."

He cupped her elbow, steadying her as she stepped up onto the sidewalk.

The touch was light and brief, but she felt it all the way to her toes. Adam would never have thought about doing anything like that. He'd always bounded ahead of her like an overexcited puppy.

Not Jacob. Jacob made her feel…treasured. Nobody had ever made her feel like that before. That was why she'd embarrassed herself by crying on the porch yesterday, when he'd insisted on checking the boards and steadying her arm. She'd forgotten for a moment that Jacob was a minister, that he was just doing his job.

That his kindness was nothing personal.

As they approached the store, Natalie noticed a wooden sign propped in the window. Relieved, she halted where she was. "Look." She pointed. "It's closed."

"Don't worry," Jacob told her. "I called the owner while you were making out your list. She's meeting us here."

"Oh, you shouldn't have done that. I don't want to be a bother." Now she'd *have* to buy something.

"Bailey doesn't mind."

A brass bell clanged when Jacob pulled open the door, and warm spiced air washed across

Natalie's face. Her heart sank. This place even smelled expensive.

The shop had the feel of an old general store, combined with a dash of quirky style. Rough plank shelves lined the walls, showcasing gleaming mason jars full of sauces and jams. Oranges and apples were tumbled into bushel baskets on a wide farmhouse table. The spicy smell wafted from a selection of bulk spices she could see in the half-opened square drawers of an old cabinet. A little glass jar of adorably tiny silver scoops stood nearby for measuring, along with a stack of small plastic bags.

It was all very trendy and cute, but she didn't see a price tag on anything. That was never a good sign.

"Bailey!" Jacob called out suddenly, making Natalie jump. "Customers!"

"Coming!" A muffled female voice answered from the back, and a slim dark-haired young woman appeared, wiping her hands with the tail of a green apron. "I was washing out some jars while I waited for you." She smiled warmly, and her gaze lingered on Natalie, a light of friendly curiosity in her bright eyes. "Welcome to Bailey's."

"Bailey Quinn, this is Natalie Davis. Like I told you, she's new in town, and she needs to pick up a few groceries."

"I'm sorry to make you open up on a Sunday," Natalie interjected quickly.

"Oh, it's nothing. Like everybody else around here, I owe the good pastor more favors than I can count. I'm always glad for the chance to pay one back. Here." Bailey rolled a child's red wagon out from behind the counter. She took three roomy wicker baskets from a stack on the floor, and nestled them neatly in its bed. "We sure don't want you carrying anything heavy, do we? Just wheel this around and gather up what you need. And take your time. I'm in no hurry at all."

Nobody in Pine Valley seemed to be in a hurry. "Thanks. You're very kind."

Bailey's perfect smile widened. "Not to get personal, but I can see you're expecting. Don't you worry. Everything here's as natural as can be. No preservatives and no chemicals. I make sure of it."

Oh dear. Natalie managed a wavering smile in return before moving off to inspect the closest shelf. This was even worse than she'd thought. She'd priced the all-natural items at her local superstore when she'd first realized she was pregnant, and she'd been shocked at the cost difference. Eating healthy wasn't cheap.

Jacob and Bailey chatted as Natalie moved slowly around the store. They seemed to know each other well. Were they a couple? Maybe that was the reason Bailey had been so quick to agree to open up. She looked like the type of woman who might be involved with a man like Jacob.

Natalie squashed a twinge of envy. Jacob Stone's personal life was none of her business, and right now she had other things to worry about. She needed to figure out how little she could actually purchase without looking ungrateful.

She ended up with a jar of spaghetti sauce, a plastic bag of wide homemade noodles, three oranges, two apples, and the smallest container of milk in the refrigerated dairy case. She looked longingly at a cellophane bag of granola, thick with dried cranberries and walnuts, all tied up with a saucy red bow. It probably cost the earth, and there was no telling what she was already spending. She put it carefully back on the shelf and walked over to the old-fashioned cash register.

Please, God. Don't let this be over thirty dollars.

"All done?" Bailey lifted the half-filled basket and set it on the counter. As she began ringing up the purchase, Jacob looked at Natalie and frowned.

"That's all you're getting?"

Natalie felt her cheeks burn hot. "For now. I told you I didn't need much."

"You don't know when your car's going to be drivable. I mean, we're hoping for an easy fix, but we can't be sure of it. You probably should buy enough for at least a couple of days."

Natalie fished for something convincing to say, but she wasn't quite quick enough. Bailey cleared her throat gently and shot a meaningful look at Jacob. Understanding flashed across his face.

"Natalie, I'm so sorry. Hold up with that total, Bailey, okay? I'll be right back."

He grabbed the handle of the little wagon, and Natalie watched in horror as he strode around the store. Another container of milk, a loaf of bread, two quarts of homemade soup, more apples, and some jars of green beans were loaded into the empty baskets. He must have noticed her ogling the granola because he tossed three bags of that in, too.

When he'd loaded the wagon with more food than she'd ever personally bought at one time, he returned to the register and began heaving the overfilled baskets onto the scarred counter.

"I don't need all that," Natalie protested weakly.

"Yes, you do. Ring it up, Bailey." He reached in his back pocket and pulled out his wallet.

When Natalie opened her mouth, he glanced at her and shook his head. "Nope. My treat."

Bailey was fighting a smile as she rang up the additional items, but Natalie had never felt so embarrassed in her life. She knew her face must be as red as the stubby fire hydrant they'd passed on their way in.

She stood by awkwardly as the cash register's bells chirped. When she heard the final total, her knees actually went weak.

Jacob handed over his credit card without a blink. "Thanks, Bailey."

"Anytime. Glad to meet you, Natalie. Welcome to Pine Valley." As Jacob gathered up the bags of groceries and headed toward the door, Bailey leaned forward, handing Natalie a pretty green-and-white business card.

"This has my cell number on it. You need anything else, just give me a call. I can even deliver if you're not feeling up to getting out. I'd like to nose around Lark Hill, anyway. Those early blueberries that grow out there are legendary around here, and they should be ready to pick soon. If you decide you want to sell any of them, let me know. I'd definitely be interested. And in the meantime, if you're a little short on cash, I can run an account for you. I do it all the time. I heard what happened at your wedding. Buying groceries should be the least of your problems."

Natalie stood rooted to the varnished floor with no idea what to say. She should have listened to Cora and stayed on the farm. This had been a big mistake.

"Thanks," she managed finally. "That's very nice of you, but I'm sure it won't be necessary." Natalie smiled, then turned and made a beeline for the door.

Jacob had the groceries stowed by the time she reached the truck. Shame, guilt and worry were churning around in Natalie's stomach like dirty clothes in a washing machine, and she felt faintly sick. She really hoped Jacob wouldn't try to talk to her on the ride home. She fixed her eyes straight ahead when he climbed in the driver's seat.

"You ready to go? Fasten your seat belt."

She'd forgotten about the stupid seat belt. She managed to get the canvas strip positioned across the fullness of her pregnant tummy, but she couldn't quite slide the metal tip into its slot. A fresh wave of embarrassment welled up within her. She was *so* tired of fumbling around like some kind of beached whale.

Jacob waited a minute or two while the truck idled noisily. Then he reached over and took the end of the belt out of her hand, clicking it smoothly into place.

"There you go," he said cheerfully.

She didn't answer. They rode all the way back to the farmhouse in complete silence. Out of the corner of her eye, she could see Jacob darting concerned glances her way, but he held his tongue.

She was being rude, and she knew it. She ought to spend this ride thanking Jacob for his generosity, not sulking like some ungrateful toddler.

Natalie had received plenty of charity in her life, and she knew exactly how she was supposed to act. She'd stood way too many times next to chiming cash registers while people she barely knew paid for her school supplies, clothes or even embarrassingly personal items like underwear.

People expected to be thanked.

And she *was* truly thankful for every person who'd helped her; she really was. But the whole point of marrying Adam and coming to Pine Valley was so that her baby would never have to grit his teeth behind a grateful smile the way Natalie had done all her childhood.

Things were supposed to be different here.

When they pulled to a stop in the yard, she immediately released the seat belt and reached for the door handle. She needed to get inside before her stupid pregnancy hormones took over and she either lost her temper or bawled like a baby.

"Wait, Natalie. Please."

Something in his voice made her stop. She froze, the door lever halfway pressed, then faced him for the first time since they'd left Bailey's.

His brows were drawn together in a troubled line, and his greenish-blue eyes searched hers. "I upset you back at the store, and I'm really sorry about that. Sometimes I jump in without thinking things through." He offered her a hopeful smile, a dimple flickering boyishly in his cheek. "I get in trouble for that a lot, actually. Please forgive me if I embarrassed you."

Natalie's irritation was washed away by a wave of pure exhaustion. He *had* embarrassed her, but she couldn't see any good that could come from pointing that out now. Anyway, she'd learned her lesson.

She wouldn't be opening the door to Jacob Stone again.

"That's okay. Buying all that…it was kind of you. It really was. I'm just…tired. I think I'm going to go in and lie down."

"I understand." He nodded slowly, that glimmer of a boyish twinkle gone. "At least let me carry the groceries in for you and help you put them away before I go."

"Thanks, but I can do it myself."

"Natalie, these bags are heavy. Let me—"

"I'll manage," she broke in firmly. "I'd really like to be alone. Could you just set the groceries on the porch, please? I'll bring them in myself."

She got out of the truck and walked as fast as she could toward the house. This time, Jacob didn't try to stop her. Once inside, she leaned against the closed door and waited until she heard his old truck crunch down the driveway.

When she peeked out, she saw that Jacob had done exactly what she'd asked. There on the porch, neatly lined up, were the brown paper bags from Bailey's. On one of them was written in a black masculine script "Really sorry."

"Bleaaah!" She glanced over to see Rufus trotting from the direction of the barn, and she felt a flutter of alarm. That goat ate everything; she'd even caught him chewing on the handle of an old hammer. He'd make short work of these expensive groceries.

She quickly dragged the bags into the living room, slamming the door in Rufus's curious face in the nick of time. She took a second to catch her breath, then began the task of carrying the food into the kitchen. The bags were even heavier than she'd expected, but she managed.

She was setting the last sack on the table when the first real pain struck.

Chapter Five

Jacob slammed his shoulder against the warped side door of the church. In spite of the sign he'd posted on the inside, somebody leaving the Sunday night prayer service had left this way. Now the door wouldn't close.

Nothing had gone right today.

He honestly hadn't meant to embarrass Natalie at the grocery store. He'd just gotten so frustrated, watching her at Bailey's, carefully examining cans and bags before putting them right back on the shelves. Like that fancy granola. She obviously wanted it, and after all Natalie had been through in the past couple of days, all the challenges she still faced, she shouldn't have to deny herself a little treat. His self-control had snapped its leash, and he'd barged in and bought the cereal, along with everything else he could think of.

He'd mishandled the whole shopping trip. The truth had dawned on him a split second after he'd asked Natalie why she'd brought so little up to the register. She didn't have enough money to buy the things she needed, not at a place like Bailey's.

He should have thought of that beforehand. But he hadn't, and he'd felt like a colossal jerk.

He didn't like that feeling, especially not where Natalie Davis was concerned. When she'd looked up at him with those hurt brown eyes, he felt like he'd just ripped the wings off a butterfly.

He was a minister, for crying out loud. He was supposed to help people, not hurt them.

Unfortunately, tonight he couldn't even close a door right. He tried again to turn the key in the lock but the thing was still too far out of square. Frustrated beyond his limits, Jacob stepped back and kicked the door as hard as he could.

"That's not going to help." Jacob turned to find Hoyt Bradley standing a few feet behind him, hands shoved into his pockets. "And I've kicked a few doors myself, so that's experience talking."

"Yeah, well, this one deserves it, trust me. You're a little late for tonight's meeting, but I'm sure glad you showed up. Can you do anything to make this shut so I can lock it?" Hoyt was the owner of Bradley Builders, and a faithful member of Pine Valley Community. If he couldn't manhandle this door back into line, nobody could.

Hoyt hesitated a second, then stepped forward. He ran practiced hands over the door, pressing gently here and there, then stepped back and shook his head. "Nothing that won't involve taking it off its hinges and rehanging it at the very least. Most likely, you're going to need a whole new door."

"Great." Jacob muttered. Adding even small repairs to the church budget right now was only going to add fuel to Digby's argument for a new building. That was the last thing Jacob needed.

His phone buzzed in his jacket pocket, but he ignored it. It had started ringing about an hour ago, right in the middle of the opening prayer. He'd forgotten to put it on vibrate before the prayer service started. Again.

Which reminded him. When he finally made it home tonight, he was changing his generic ringtone to something a little more dignified than the theme from *Star Wars*.

Not that it had mattered much. Hardly anybody had been there to hear the goofy music. Attendance tonight had been pitiful, barely half what they usually had.

Hoyt's seat had been one of the empty ones,

and that was very unusual. A recent widower and a single dad, Hoyt was leaning pretty heavily on his faith these days. Jacob turned his attention to the builder.

"We missed you tonight."

"Yeah. About that." Hoyt shifted uncomfortably. "That's why I stopped by, as a matter of fact."

Something about Hoyt's tone put Jacob on high alert. "Is that so?"

The builder nodded. "Truth is, I owe you an apology, and I didn't want to waste any time before coming out here and giving it to you."

"I doubt it, but what for?"

"I'm figuring I wasn't the only person who didn't make it to the prayer meeting tonight. I know that because I was with the rest of them… most of them anyway…at Digby Markham's place. Digby invited me because they were going to talk about this fellowship hall deal."

"Ah." Jacob nodded slowly.

"I knew you weren't too gung ho about it, but a fellowship hall like they're talking about would be a big contract for me. And the way things are, not too many people are building here right now, so business is slow. I have to look out for my guys. A project like that could keep all my men busy for months. Most of them have families to take care of, and they need that money. I'm sorry, Jacob, but I just didn't feel like I could pass up the chance to sit in on any meeting that might land me the contract."

"I see." He considered Hoyt a friend, so yeah, it stung a little that he'd crossed over to Digby's side. But he couldn't fault the man's reasoning. Work was scarce. "You don't owe me any apology for looking out for your workers, Hoyt."

"That's not what I'm apologizing for." The builder drew in a deep breath. "If that's all the meeting had been about, I wouldn't be here. But there was a good bit more going on. Did you know Digby has a nephew who's a preacher?"

Jacob's heart sank. "I'd heard that, yes."

"Well, he was at the meeting, too, him and his wife. It was plain to me from the get-go that Digby's hoping to get him your job here at the church. I didn't have a clue that was in the wind, or I wouldn't have ever gone over there, contract or no contract. I want you to know that."

So Arlene was right. She usually was. "It's okay, Hoyt."

"No, it isn't. You were there for me and my family when Marylee got sick…and later when she passed on. And not just at the start of it. You kept coming, kept just *being* there with us. You never stopped, even when I wasn't…handling things so well. Remember?"

Jacob remembered. Those had been some

dark days. "Nobody handles things like that well, Hoyt."

"You did," the contractor said simply. "And I owe you for it. I haven't forgotten. Digby's playing some dirty pool. Building a fellowship hall's one thing. I could see that, if the church can come up with the money. But the other... well, I want no part of it, and I'm sorry I went to that meeting. That's why I came out here tonight. I wanted to tell you about it." The builder held out his hand. "I hope you'll forgive me."

Jacob clasped the man's roughened hand firmly. "There's nothing to forgive, Hoyt."

"So we're good, then."

"Yeah. We're good."

"That's all I needed to know. I'll stop by tomorrow and take some measurements on this door. I'll see to it for you, no charge. But there's not much I can do about it tonight, I'm afraid."

"Doesn't matter. I think we've both had enough for one night. As far as I'm concerned, if anybody can pry this thing open, they're more than welcome to help themselves to whatever they can find inside."

"Fair enough." Hoyt nodded, clapped Jacob hard on the back, then headed back toward the street and his hulking work truck. Jacob watched the other man go for a second or two, before turning toward the parking lot where his own truck waited.

He'd head back to his empty apartment, nuke a frozen burrito and spend the rest of the evening trying to decide out how best to deal with this latest development in the ongoing Digby debacle.

He wished there was somebody he could talk this over with, but it wasn't something he should share with anybody else in his congregation. After all, Digby Markham was a member of Pine Valley Community, too, and for now, at least, Jacob was his pastor.

He'd have to figure it out on his own.

Jacob flipped up the collar of his jacket as he walked across the darkened church lawn. The air's unseasonable chill added to his general feeling of discouragement. He'd be glad when this crazy cold spell broke. Winter had dragged on way past its expiration date, and he was tired of it.

He was ready for something different.

Something better.

And that was true of more than just the weather. He was also deep down bone weary of being alone.

That had dragged on for a long time, too.

It had been years now since he'd had somebody special in his life, somebody to bring flowers to or try out a new restaurant with. Somebody who'd tease him when he'd gone too long without a haircut, somebody with access to the one part of his heart that he kept strictly private.

This solitary lifestyle was supposed to be temporary. One day, he'd told himself, his workload would settle down, he'd find the right woman and he'd trade in this makeshift bachelor life for the adventure of marriage.

In spite of valiant matchmaking attempts by the women of his congregation, that hadn't happened. The woman he was looking for—the one who would bring that spark to his heart that nobody else could—had just never come along. So here he was, still stuck in the same old rut, dealing with church feuds, clogged-up nursery plumbing and a chronic case of indigestion from the frozen dinners that he ate alone late at night in his apartment. His life sure didn't feel particularly adventurous right now.

It just felt empty.

As he fished in his jacket pocket for the truck keys, his phone buzzed against his fingertips like an angry bee. He pulled out the device and checked the screen. That unknown number again. He'd better go ahead and answer because this was either a really persistent telemarketer or some kind of emergency.

"Hello?"

"Jacob?" The feminine voice on the other end of the line sounded strained.

"Natalie? What's going on? Are you okay?"

"I'm…so sorry…to bother you." She seemed to be breathing oddly. "But I don't know anybody else to call…and the baby—"

Jacob had never really understood before what it felt like to have your blood run cold. Now he did. She was alone out there with no car, and she was desperate enough that she'd called him for help. Repeatedly.

Starting almost an hour ago.

"I'm on my way. Just sit tight." He jumped inside the truck and squealed out of the church parking lot on two tires.

By the time he'd pulled up in front of Lark Hill, he'd set a new personal record for undetected traffic violations. He'd also figured out the quickest way to Fairmont Medical Center. It was the closest hospital to Pine Valley, and no matter how many different routes he considered, a good thirty-five minutes away.

Leaving the truck running, he raced to the door. She met him there, dragging her pink overnight case behind her and cradling her round stomach with her free hand. In the faint light from the dim porch bulb, her face looked tense.

"I'll take that." He scooped up the suitcase

with one hand and took her arm with the other. "Come on, now. Nice and slow. No need to hurry. We'll get you to the hospital in plenty of time."

He hoped he was telling her the truth about that.

Please, God, get us there with time to spare. Lots of time. Hours and hours of time. No near misses tonight, all right? If it's all the same to You, I'd really rather not deliver this baby on the side of the road.

He helped her carefully into the truck and scrambled into the driver's seat. As they barreled down the driveway, he saw Rufus, loose again, spotlighted in the headlights. Jacob didn't even slow down. He lay on the horn and swerved, whizzing past the animal.

"When did the pains start?" That was the question he was supposed to ask, right? And something about how far apart they were.

Unfortunately, he couldn't remember what any of the potential answers meant.

"Right after you left."

He took his eyes off the road long enough to stare at her. "But that was hours ago."

"I know. I… I wasn't sure at first. And then when I called…"

When she'd called, he hadn't answered. After all his offers of help, all his assurances, she'd had to call him four times to tell him she was in labor.

Four stinking times.

"I'm so sorry I missed your calls, Natalie. I was in the middle of a prayer meeting, and I had no idea."

She didn't answer. When he looked over, he guessed by the look of pained concentration on her face that she was having a contraction. He pressed his foot down harder on the gas pedal.

He'd never felt so relieved in his life as he did half an hour later when they pulled up into the brightly lit hospital parking lot.

Thank You, Lord. Thank You, thank You, thank You.

The grateful refrain echoed in his head as he parked the truck in front of the emergency room entrance. Then he hesitated, unsure what he was supposed to do next.

"Do you want me to go in and get you a wheelchair or something? Or do you want to walk?" He didn't know what the protocol was at this point. All he knew was that he was ready to turn Natalie over to a fully competent medical professional and collapse somewhere in a relieved heap.

And if he never lived through another day like this one, it would be way too soon.

"I can walk." Natalie reached for the door

handle, and he noticed that her hand was shaking. "Thank you very much for driving me."

"Whoa. Wait there." Even he knew that a pregnant lady didn't walk into the hospital by herself.

"Thanks, but I've already bothered you enough. I'll be fine."

Jacob started to argue, but he remembered the disaster at Bailey's earlier and stopped. He couldn't just keep pushing himself into this woman's personal business without her permission. He had to respect her wishes, whether he wanted to or not.

Natalie hesitated, her hand resting on the door handle, looking through the truck window at the brightly lit building. She bit her lip and turned to look back at him. "This is…a good hospital, though? For new babies? They'll take really good care of him?"

"It's a great hospital, and they'll take really good care of both of you." That was true enough, but Jacob's mind wasn't on his words.

Natalie's face was pale, her mouth was trembling and there was a wide, blank look in her eyes. She was doing her best to hide it, but she was scared to death. And why wouldn't she be? She was in labor with her first baby, in a strange place where she knew nobody.

As he watched, she swallowed hard, nodded

and started to open the door. "All right, then. Thanks again for the ride."

"I was happy to do it. And I'm so sorry I didn't answer my phone the first time you called."

"That's okay. I understand. After…how I acted about the groceries this afternoon, I was surprised you answered it at all. But I'm very grateful you did."

Jacob frowned as realization struck him.

She'd been afraid he wouldn't come to help her. When he hadn't picked up the phone right away, she'd assumed he was deliberately brushing off her calls.

His mind skimmed over what that must have felt like, being alone on that old farm, in pain, frightened, having to turn to someone you barely knew—someone who'd embarrassed you royally just that afternoon—in order to get a ride to the hospital. And then having him not answer your repeated calls for help.

Jacob felt slightly sick. That did it.

He'd respect this woman's boundaries another day, every single one of them. He'd stay politely on the other side of whatever fence she wanted to put up between them.

But not tonight. Tonight, like it or not, she was stuck with him.

Okay, God. Feel free to jump in here anytime

with some guidance because I think things are about to get really interesting.

"I'm staying with you." He jumped out of the truck before she could protest and bounded around to the passenger door.

"No," she said as soon as he opened it. "I can't ask you to—"

"You didn't ask. I offered." He reached behind her and snagged her little suitcase. "Okay now, take my arm, and let's go nice and slow."

She was shaking her head. "You don't have to stay. I can handle this by myself."

Jacob knew a bluff when he heard one. She wasn't nearly as sure of that as she was trying to sound. "Sure you can. But you're not going to." Their gazes locked. "I'm staying, Natalie. Either right beside you in the labor room or in the closest waiting room. That's your choice. But I'm staying right here at this hospital until this baby is born."

He could see her fear tussling with her reluctance to accept his help. The fear won. "I... guess that would be...nice. If you're sure you don't mind. But just for a little while. I don't want to keep you too long."

"I've got nothing else to do tonight. Nothing this exciting, anyway." That much was certainly true. "I'm not going anywhere."

And he didn't, for what turned out to be one of the most memorable nights of his life.

He sat beside her in the labor room, watching helplessly as the contractions intensified. He had no idea what to do, but she seemed okay with him sitting beside her. So that's what he did. Hour after hour after hour.

One thing was for sure. He shouldn't have worried about her having the baby on the ride to the hospital. Babies took forever.

As the night wore on, he lost track of time. He lost track of everything except the rhythm of the contractions and the beep of the monitors. He learned to tell when a pain was starting by the expression on Natalie's face and learned with the help of the nurses how to help her breathe her way through it. She liked the lights dim, he discovered, and so whenever the nurses left the room, he flicked off the glaring overhead light. For the first three or four hours, she thanked him quietly each time. After that, she was past words, but she didn't protest when he took her hand in his so she could squeeze it during the contractions.

His sense of anticipation built hour by hour as the baby's arrival inched closer. He'd been beside countless hospital beds in his time, but mostly it was for the end of life, not for the beginning.

It was a nice change to be waiting for somebody's first breath rather than the last.

Finally, the gray-haired head nurse glanced his way and smiled. "Time to kick you out, Pastor. This baby's about ready to make his entrance." Jacob had just finished coaching Natalie through a fierce contraction, and he blinked at the nurse, her words not quite registering. "Go on, now," she urged. "Scat. We need to get down to business in here, and I don't think you're invited to this part of the party."

"Oh! Right." He glanced down at Natalie. Her hair was damp with perspiration, but she managed to smile up at him.

He wasn't even surprised. If he'd learned one thing over the past hours, it was that Natalie Davis, small and dainty as she was, had more courage and stamina than anybody he'd ever met.

She seemed to want to say something, so he leaned in closer.

"Th-thank you, Jacob," she panted, her pain-glazed brown eyes looking up into his. "F-for staying."

His throat closed, and he blinked furiously. "You're very welcome. I'll be just outside. Okay? Right outside that door, if you need me."

She was already in the grip of another contraction, and he wasn't sure if she heard him or not. Two more nurses and a white-coated doctor brushed past him into the room as he stepped out, and he heard the excited chatter behind him go up a few decibels before the door glided closed.

After all those hours of waiting, things were finally starting to happen. And here he was, stuck on the wrong side of this stupid door. He fought an urge to kick it.

But he'd already kicked enough doors for one night, and anyway, he was exactly where he belonged. He wasn't Natalie's husband. This deeply intimate experience wasn't his to share. He had no right to feel disappointed that he didn't get to participate in the miraculous joy of the baby's actual birth.

Just down the hall was a waiting room crowded with expectant grandparents and excited relatives. He could walk down there and find himself a seat. Check his cell phone for messages. Reconnect with his own life and responsibilities.

He *could* do that. But he didn't.

Instead, he stayed right where he was, leaning against the beige wall, trying to pray, and straining his ears to hear what was going on in the room behind him. He was still standing there, nearly an hour later, when he heard the baby's first shaky wail.

Then for the second time in twenty-four hours, he found himself silently praying the same words over and over.

Thank You, Lord. Thank You, thank You, thank You.

A rhythmic creaking noise woke her. Natalie opened her eyes, and creamy yellow walls with decals of flowers and butterflies swam into focus.

That's right. She was in the hospital maternity ward, and her son, Ethan, was here, almost three weeks ahead of schedule.

She turned her head toward the clear bassinet the nurses had brought in last night. It was empty, but she didn't have to look far to find her baby.

Jacob Stone was in the rocking chair in front of the big window, holding Ethan swaddled in a pale blue blanket. It made a sweet picture, the broad-shouldered man cradling the sleeping baby gently in his arms. Natalie's heart overflowed with a confusing mix of gratitude and pain.

The scene in front of her was beautiful—and sad.

If things were as they ought to be, her husband would be sitting there. He'd be the man with tired lines around the corners of his eyes, hair tousled. He'd be the one worn-out from breathing with her through contractions all last night, but still up and rocking their son with the rapt attention of a brand-new daddy.

As much as she wanted to believe that would have happened if Adam had gone through with their wedding, the idea was hard to square with the guy she knew.

A memory flitted through her mind. Once, at the beginning of their relationship, Adam had driven her to the emergency room because she'd become dehydrated from battling a stomach virus. A few minutes after they'd arrived, he'd left her in the waiting room in search of a vending machine. He'd told her he was going to buy himself a pack of crackers and a Coke. He'd be back in five minutes.

He'd vanished for an hour and a half.

When he'd reappeared, he'd had a great story to tell about a Jamaican radiologist he'd met in the elevator. The two men had ended up talking about mountain climbing over coffee and pie in the basement cafeteria.

That was Adam.

Last night, as her contractions had come closer and harder, Jacob had asked the nurse for a washcloth, which he'd dampened and dabbed lightly against her sweaty forehead. He'd patiently kept his position at her side for hour after hour, never complaining, never looking for an excuse to leave the room. At one point, when Jacob was spooning more ice chips into her dry mouth, she'd actually found herself feeling thankful, not only that Jacob had insisted on staying with her, but that *he* was the one beside her instead of Adam. And later, when the new night nurse had assumed Jacob was her husband, Natalie had found herself wishing it was true.

But just like those gourmet groceries at Bailey's, wishes like those were out of her price range. No point making herself even sadder by pining for the impossible.

Now that the baby was here, Adam would be coming back. They'd be getting married, and starting their new life together. She needed to focus on that.

"You're awake." Jacob's voice startled her out of her thoughts. "How are you feeling?"

She forced a smile. "Better than I would have thought, actually." She levered herself up on her elbows and winced.

"Whoa, there. Stay still. I'll put Ethan down and show you how that bed works."

She watched as he placed the sleeping newborn into the bassinet, tucking the tail of the soft blanket around him. The baby's eyelids fluttered briefly, and he worked his rosebud of a mouth for a second. Then the tiny lips sagged apart, and he was deeply asleep again.

Natalie felt a rush of love. Her son was absolutely perfect.

"See?" Jacob was fiddling with her bed rail. "If you press that button right there, you can raise up the back and get yourself comfortable." She followed his instructions, and the bed whirred into gear. The noise sounded loud in the quiet room, and she threw an alarmed look in the baby's direction. Jacob laughed.

"Don't worry. He's zonked. Our Ethan's a great little sleeper."

Our Ethan. A fresh wave of confused longings rose up in her, feelings she had no idea what to do with. She'd be so glad when her hormones settled down and she was able to think straight again.

"You've been sleeping pretty well yourself." Jacob smiled at her. "I'm glad. You earned it. You were really brave."

"Not me." Natalie shook her head. "I was scared to death."

"Of course you were. But you hung in there like a champ, anyway. Nope," he said as Natalie started to speak. "No arguing. I was there. I saw it. Give yourself some credit, Natalie. You were amazing."

The unexpected praise made tears well up in

her eyes. Before she could think of a good reply, somebody rapped briskly on the hospital door.

A nurse in teddy bear scrubs came in, wheeling a stand hung with various bits of medical equipment. "I'm Stacy, and I'm here to check your vitals, Miss Davis. And Miss Patty's bringing up a special delivery for you."

"I think I've already had one of those," Natalie said, smiling at the baby snuggled in his little plastic bubble.

The young dark-haired nurse laughed. "This one's not half so sweet, but it's a good bit less trouble to get." She'd crossed back to hold the door open.

Natalie's eyes widened. The entire upper half of the doorway was filled with flowers: pink roses, white carnations and sprays of baby's breath, accented with glossy green ferns. Their sweet scent wafted over her as the huge bouquet wobbled forward into the room, propelled by a pair of plump legs in white support hose.

An elderly hospital volunteer poked her head around the bobbing blooms. "Where do you want me to put these, dearie?"

"I…uh…" Natalie stuttered. She wasn't sure. She'd never gotten flowers before.

Ever.

"I'll take them, Miss Patty." Jacob relieved

the older woman of her burden and settled the arrangement on the wide windowsill.

"Thanks." The volunteer sighed and brushed a few stray petals off the front of her pink smock. "That's the heaviest bouquet I've ever toted, and thanks to this here card I know just who to blame. I do believe you're trying to kill me, Pastor Stone."

"I'm not trying to kill you, Miss Patty. I'm trying to reform you. And if a little hard labor won't do that, what will? But just so we stay on speaking terms, I'll help you make the rest of your deliveries this morning. I probably need to give Stacy some elbow room in here, anyway. If—" Jacob paused, looking over at Natalie with one eyebrow raised "—that's all right with you?"

Natalie had to answer with a nod. She wasn't sure she could speak. Her heart had jumped up and lodged itself somewhere in her throat.

Jacob had sent her flowers.

"I'll be back in about half an hour," Jacob promised her as he held the door open for the pink lady. "I've got my cell phone if you need anything." He winked as he followed the older woman out into the corridor, still teasing. "The florist told me there'd be balloons with those, Miss Patty. Are you stealing balloons again? Because we talked about that."

Natalie didn't hear the volunteer's reply, but whatever it was, it must have been funny because Jacob's laugh echoed down the hall.

Even Stacy was chuckling as she fastened the blood pressure cuff around Natalie's upper arm. "That man is something else."

"He is," Natalie agreed. "He's certainly been very kind to me, even though I've put him to an awful lot of trouble."

"Oh, I wouldn't worry about that, if I were you. Jacob's used to it." The nurse frowned as she tapped in some numbers on the little tablet she carried. "He's always doing something for somebody, that one. Of course, that's kind of his job, isn't it? Being he's a minister, I mean."

Natalie's heart dropped slowly from her throat down into the pit of her stomach. That's right. He was.

She'd almost forgotten.

"Not that he's pushy about it, mind you." The nurse rounded the bed, leaned over the bassinet and began to unwrap Ethan's swaddling. "Some of the preachers that come here are, but never Jacob. He just sees what folks need done and does it. It seems to work. I've lost count of the patients who've ended up attending his church. Nurses, too." She finished checking Ethan over and began deftly rewrapping the squirming baby. "Of course, it doesn't hurt any that he's so easy on the eyes, does it? I'd go over there myself if I wasn't so happy in my own church. Do you attend Pine Valley Community, Miss Davis?"

"No." Natalie's answer sounded so flat that the nurse glanced up from her tablet, her eyebrows lifted curiously.

"I'm sorry. I didn't mean to assume anything. You aren't a Christian?"

"Yes, I'm a believer, I'm just…not much of a church person, I guess."

"Is that so?" The nurse tilted her head and flashed a little smile. "Well, you never know. A minister like Jacob Stone might just change your mind about that."

Chapter Six

Two days later, Jacob was standing in front of the parenting books in Pine Valley's only bookstore, his cell phone pressed to his ear. He was doing his best to keep his voice down. He didn't like having a personal conversation in a public place like Pages, but as usual, Digby Markham hadn't given him much choice.

"You're supposed to request permission from the board *before* you make purchases, Jacob. But in this case, even if you had, there's no way we'd reimburse you for those groceries."

"I'm not asking you to." Jacob pulled another book out of the new baby section and glanced at its cover. He added it to the growing stack by his feet.

"You sent in the bill for reimbursement."

"I already told you—that was a mistake." Arlene had swiped the receipt off his desk in one of her cleaning frenzies and added it to the expense folder that she submitted monthly to the church board for repayment. Digby had promptly hit the roof, and Jacob had been stuck on the phone listening to a lecture on the proper stewardship of church finances for the last ten minutes.

It was getting old, and it didn't appear to be winding down.

"And I've already told *you*, the church's benevolence fund is strictly for members of our own congregation. My understanding is you were buying those groceries for that pregnant woman who got dumped at her wedding. Thankfully, *she* isn't associated with our church in any way."

Jacob froze, his index finger on the spine of a book entitled *Mothering Made Easy.* "Thankfully?"

"You know what I mean."

"Being a good steward of God's money means using it wisely, not piling it up and sitting on it. Especially when we see our neighbors in need." He knew he was wasting his breath, but he couldn't help it. Digby was pushing all his buttons today.

"As a banker, I think I know a little more about managing money than you do." Digby snorted. "You can waste your own money however you like, but I can't allow your irresponsible spending to deplete the church's funds, especially not right now."

Because of that fellowship hall you want to build. Jacob struggled to rein in his temper. To be fair, Digby had at least one valid point buried in there. Jacob did tend to open his wallet without considering the consequences and the skimpy balances in his personal checking and savings accounts bore testimony to that fact.

"I have no doubt you know more about money management than I do, Digby, and I do appreciate your willingness to serve on the church board. Since I don't want repayment for the groceries, there's nothing else for us to discuss."

"There is, as it happens, just one more thing I wanted to mention to you." Something about Digby's smug tone made Jacob pause.

This couldn't be good.

"What's that?"

"I just got off the phone with our youngest board member, Darren Ellerbee. He called the bank about getting some financing for the new home he and his wife would like to buy. One thing led to another, and we had a nice long chat. I'm happy to report that he's decided to vote yes on the new fellowship hall." That made seven votes out of twelve. Jacob's heart sank. "So it appears the fellowship hall will be going forward, Stone. This building project is now the church's primary focus, at least for the foreseeable future. And from this moment on, it should be yours, as well."

Jacob closed his eyes and pressed his forehead against the sharp edge of the wooden bookcase.

He knew it would do no good, but he had to try one last time. "There's a lot more to a church than the building it meets in, Digby. Or there should be. I can't just set aside all our ongoing ministries so I can spend hours sitting at a conference table looking at blueprints and carpet swatches."

"You can, and you will. Tying up your loose ends shouldn't take more than a few days. After that, the board will expect to have your undivided attention. Prepare your sermons and visit our congregation's shut-ins and all that, certainly. In moderation. But otherwise, you are to make this building project your top priority until it is completed."

"But that could take a year."

"Oh, it'll take far longer than that. We're not talking about slapping together some kind of low-budget building. We want to build the sort of fellowship hall that will draw more of the *right sort* of people into our church." Digby chuckled grimly. "I promise you, once we get this facility up and running, Good Shepherd won't know what hit them. They haven't up-dated that annex of theirs in decades."

Jacob sighed. Yep. Definitely time to recycle that *Same Team* sermon. "Isn't a building like that a little out of our price range, though?"

"Not if we're smart it won't be. That's why there are to be absolutely no more unauthorized expenditures of any kind during this time. We need to be funneling money into our accounts, not siphoning it out. In fact, I'll need to start setting up fund-raising meetings right away."

More meetings. Jacob managed not to groan out loud, but it was a near thing.

It didn't matter. Digby continued as if he'd read Jacob's mind. "And you will attend every single one of them, Pastor Stone. Also, you'll be required to take the lead in our fund-raising ef-forts. After all the unnecessary delay and argu-ment about this matter, the congregation needs to see that you are fully on board with this en-deavor."

"But I'm not on board, Digby. Fully or oth-erwise."

"Then I suggest you *get* on board. Immedi-ately."

"Or what?" Jacob asked the question quietly, but a lot hung in the balance of Digby's answer.

There was a heavy tick of silence before the

church board chairman spoke again. "Or we'll find a minister who will. Good day, Pastor Stone."

Jacob disconnected the call and fought the urge to hurl his phone at the wall.

So that was that. Digby couldn't have made it any plainer.

Either he fell meekly in line about the fellowship hall project, or he was out of a job. The worst thing was, he had nobody to blame for this situation but himself. The banker had been only asked to serve on the church board after Jacob's impulsive enthusiasm for helping people had outrun the church's resources one time too many.

Some things never changed. He mentally tallied up the cost of the books he'd chosen for Natalie, blanched and regretfully put all but one back on the shelf. His checking account was running on fumes right now, and he'd have to watch it if he was going to make ends meet until payday.

He carried the book he'd chosen to the checkout counter and braced himself for yet another uncomfortable conversation. Anna Delaney wasn't much for gossip, but still. There was no way an unmarried minister was buying a parenting book in Pine Valley without offering some kind of explanation.

To his surprise, Anna only nodded. "Good

choice. This is the most popular one with the new moms right now. She'll love it." She caught his eye and smiled. "Don't look so surprised. The woman's fiancé climbed out a window on her wedding day, and the town's bachelor minister ended up being her labor coach. Even I hear about things like *that*."

Jacob's heart sank. People were already gossiping, which meant he'd have Arlene on his case pretty soon. She was as protective of the church's reputation as Digby was of its bank account.

Jacob considered his debit card, tucked it back in its slot and pulled cash out of his wallet. He'd brown-bag his lunch this week.

"No charge." Anna waved away his money as she popped the book in a bag.

He shook his head. The bookstore was struggling to stay open, and he knew it. "Anna—"

"Please. I want to help. I'm sorry, but I couldn't help overhearing part of your conversation just then. Don't you pay any attention to what Digby Markham says. I think you're exactly right about what our church is supposed to be doing with its money. Besides, I owe you a lot more than the price of a book. You've been so wonderful about visiting my dad, even now that he doesn't recognize you most of the time." She swallowed hard. "I can't really pay you back, but at least I can pay the kindness forward a little bit. Right?"

Jacob's troubled heart warmed. That was the kind of thing he loved to hear from the members of his church. "How is Roger doing?"

She sighed. "Oh, you know how Alzheimer's is. He has good days and bad days, but I have to say his bad days are getting worse."

"I'll stop by soon and spend some time with him."

"I think maybe you'd better keep on doing just what you're doing, Pastor Stone. That girl needs you more than my father does right now. After all—" Anna offered him his bagged-up book and a sad smile "—Dad's got me to help him. She doesn't seem to have anybody."

As Jacob walked back to his office, he pondered the two very different conversations he'd just had. They were pretty good examples of the mind-sets dividing up his congregation right now. With this fellowship hall project gaining speed, he was going to have his hands full keeping a full-blown church split from happening.

If he could even hang on to his job, that was.

He'd been praying about all this for weeks, but so far he hadn't sensed any clear direction.

When Jacob finally slid into his truck in the church's parking lot, he sat on the sun-warmed vinyl seat and considered the simple white-steepled church in front of him. He didn't have God's answer, not yet. But he knew one would come.

Sooner or later.

In the meantime, he'd do what he always did. The next thing.

Digby had suggested he take a few days to tie up loose ends with his ongoing projects. Fine. That's exactly what he would do.

He glanced at his watch. Arlene would be at her Senior Yoga class at the community center right now. Perfect.

"Call Arlene," he instructed his phone. When his secretary's voice mail gave its go-ahead beep, he said, "Arlene, it's Jacob. I'm taking some of those vacation days you're always badgering me about, and I'll be out of the office for the rest of this week. Call Fred Parsons and get him to lead the Wednesday-night program. No calls except for emergencies, please. Thanks. I'll see you Sunday."

He ended the call. Done. He'd just arranged for the longest stretch of time off work he'd had since he'd graduated from seminary.

As a precaution, he set the phone on vibrate before he stuck it back into his shirt pocket. Senior Yoga only lasted another thirty minutes. As soon as Arlene heard his message, she'd be blowing up his phone, wanting details.

He didn't intend to give them.

Jacob sat still for another few seconds, watching a strong wind buffet the solemn old oaks that surrounded the church. The weather was shifting. From the look of things, either spring was finally getting started or a monster storm was headed their way. Only time would tell.

He cranked the truck and turned back toward town. He needed to make one quick stop at the bank before he headed for the two-lane highway connecting Pine Valley and Fairmont. He'd been looking forward to stopping by the hospital to see Natalie and Ethan, but that was going to have to wait for a couple of hours.

He had a little shopping to do.

"I've seen a lot of cute going-home outfits, but I think this one's the sweetest yet." In the hospital elevator, the gray-haired nurse leaned over the car seat settled in Natalie's lap and stroked the smocking on Ethan's blue romper with a gentle finger. "Hard to believe a man bought it." The woman winked at Natalie. "And that flower arrangement of yours was the biggest one on the whole maternity floor, just so you know. I'm surprised you don't want to take it home with you."

"Oh no. I'd rather leave it at the nurse's station for you all to enjoy," Natalie protested quickly.

Although it *had* been a little hard to leave those roses behind. Nobody had ever bought her flowers before. Adam certainly hadn't.

All the more reason to leave them. Now that she'd texted him that his son was born, surely Adam would be cutting his hiking trip short. He'd be coming back and taking over the role that Jacob had so kindly filled while he was gone.

And that, Natalie told herself firmly, was a good thing.

Pastor Jacob Stone had been an answer to her prayers, no doubt about it. But hopefully, this ride home from the hospital was the last favor she'd have to ask him for.

When the nurse wheeled her to the hospital's entrance, Jacob's truck was already rattling noisily at the curb. He jumped out to take charge of Ethan, fastening the car seat to some sort of a base he'd already installed in the back seat of his truck. As he did, he joked with the nurse and the security guard, who laughed and teased him right back. He seemed to know everybody, and they all seemed to like him.

And why not? He was a great guy.

He just wasn't *her* great guy.

When Jacob finished snapping in Ethan's seat, Natalie got out of the obligatory wheelchair and slid in the back of the truck beside her son. Jacob made no comment about her choice; he just settled her suitcase beside her and pulled the vehicle carefully out of the parking lot.

The truck's noisy engine would have made conversation difficult anyway, but Jacob stayed very quiet on the ride back to Pine Valley, his knuckles white on the steering wheel.

When he pulled the truck to a stop in front of the old farmhouse, he blew out a relieved breath. "I haven't felt so nervous driving since I was sixteen and taking the test for my license. I felt like I was transporting a load of nitroglycerine. This baby stuff is harder than I thought."

"Tell me about it." Natalie was struggling to release the carrier section of Ethan's car seat. "I can't even get this thing unfastened."

"Whoever designed it probably has some fancy engineering degree and no kids. But it was the highest rated one for safety. I made the store clerk check. Here, let me help you."

He hurried around the truck just as Natalie managed to press the right button. "Got it."

"I'll take him inside. The doctor said you shouldn't be carrying anything heavy for a while." He helped her out of the cramped back seat, then leaned back in to get Ethan.

As he did, she caught another whiff of the spicy scent that always clung to him, and her heartbeat sped up. That smell was uniquely Jacob's, and it was only detectable when he was very close. She'd noticed it on that first day, when he'd sat beside her to break the news about Adam and again when he'd held her hand during the long night of her labor.

That scent carried strong memories with it now, and it managed to unsettle and reassure her all at the same time. She suddenly had a wildly inappropriate desire to bury her nose in the hollow of Jacob's neck, shut out the world and breathe in the security this man seemed to carry around with him like a warm blanket.

None of that, she told herself firmly.

She heard a noise and turned to see Rufus casually rounding the corner of the house, a twig dangling out of his mouth.

"Oh man. You've got to be kidding me." Jacob straightened up. Ethan, snugly cradled in his heavy padded seat, swung easily from the minister's muscled arm. "I spent hours fixing that fence. I even made Hoyt double-check it for me. We thought for sure we had it goat-proofed this time."

Natalie's gaze had strayed over to the front porch. "Hoyt? Who's that?"

"Hoyt Bradley. He goes to our church, and he's the best general contractor in town." Jacob sent Rufus a narrow-eyed glare, and the goat backed up slowly behind the house until only the tip of his nose was visible. "Yeah, you better hide, buddy. As soon as I get this baby settled, you're going straight back in your pen."

"Jacob? What else did Hoyt do while he was here?"

Jacob glanced back at her. "I had him replace a few boards on the porch."

Natalie blinked. A few boards? This Hoyt Bradley had done a lot more than that. New wood gleamed on the steps and the porch floor, strong and golden in the afternoon sunlight.

"I'm not so sure that was a good idea. This isn't even my house, Jacob."

"There was no way you could carry a baby up and down those steps, Natalie. They were nearly rotted through. It wouldn't have been safe."

He had a point, and the fact that he cared enough to see about it for her made those silly emotional flutters start up again. *He's just doing his job*, she reminded herself firmly. *Don't read anything into it.* "I guess you're right. But how much did it cost?"

"Don't worry about that. I tried to pay Bradley, but he wouldn't hear of it. He even donated the lumber."

"Let me guess. This Hoyt owed you a favor." Everybody else in town sure seemed to. Her eyes wandered back over the porch. An elephant could walk on that thing now. "Must have been a pretty big one."

"Hoyt's wife died a couple of years ago. It was a rough time for him. I did what I could, but it wasn't all that much, to tell you the truth. He does seem to feel like he owes me, though. I don't know why. Like I said, he goes to my church."

Natalie nodded slowly. "And you were just doing your job."

Jacob smiled. "Exactly. Now let's get this little guy inside so I can go deal with that Houdini of a goat."

Jacob was glad Natalie dropped the issue of the porch repairs. He figured he'd have enough to deal with when she saw what he'd done to the *inside* of the house.

As it turned out, he was right about that.

"What…what did you do?" Five minutes later, Natalie stood in the doorway of the smaller of the farmhouse's two bedrooms, her face bewildered. "Where did all this come from?"

"The little guy needed a nursery." Jacob set Ethan, still asleep in his bucket seat, on the round blue rug he'd unrolled earlier this morning. He looked around with a rising sense of satisfaction. "And I didn't get all that much. Just the basics."

He had that on good authority. The salesclerk at the Baby Superstore in Fairmont had assured him that this was the absolute minimum for a functional baby's room. A crib, a changing table, a rocking chair and a little chest of drawers for clothes.

And airplanes. Airplanes everywhere.

When she'd asked him what theme he wanted, he hadn't had a clue what she was talking about until she explained. Apparently, all nurseries required decorations, and there seemed to be endless possibilities. He'd been in a hurry, so he'd just pointed to an airplane display. Why not? He liked airplanes.

So Ethan had airplane bedding for his crib, an airplane lamp, a rug with a big red airplane in the middle of it and a mobile of little stuffed biplanes flying in circles. The clerk had also set him up with some diapers, a baby monitor and an assortment of clothes, including some impossibly tiny socks.

He'd had no idea socks even came in a size that small. They barely fit on his thumbs.

He'd learned more—and had more fun—doing that shopping than he'd had since he'd gone on his short-term mission trip to Uganda two years ago.

And he hadn't thought about Digby or his nephew or the fellowship hall for hours.

Win-win, in his book.

"Jacob." Natalie started, then stopped and looked around at the nursery again. "This is... so generous. But I can't...there's just no way...."

He'd expected this reaction, and he had his argument all ready. "You had to have a baby bed, Natalie. Where was Ethan going to sleep? In a drawer?"

"I don't know." Her cheeks flushed. "I was going to make do somehow while I saved up for a secondhand crib. Used baby furniture is pretty easy to find." She crossed the small room and traced a finger across the polished wood of the crib he'd chosen. "Anyway, this is a lot more than just a baby bed. This stuff is all brand-new, and it looks expensive." She turned to him and took a careful breath. "It's just beautiful, Jacob, and I really appreciate all the time you took and everything. But I'm sorry. There's just no way I can accept this."

Time to pull out argument number two. "It's not for you, though. It's for Ethan. Call it a belated birthday present." He smiled at her hopefully, but Natalie's worried frown remained stubbornly in place.

"It's too much."

Jacob looked around the nursery again. Okay. Maybe he *had* gone a little bit overboard.

After cashing in some of his retirement savings at the bank, he'd driven to the baby store planning to buy one nice, sturdy crib and maybe a rocking chair. Then he'd walked into the bright store crammed with glossy baby things, and he'd decided to get Ethan a little more than that.

Somehow a little more had turned into a lot more.

He'd had a few qualms when he'd had to make two trips to haul his purchases back here in the bed of his truck. But somewhere in the back of his mind, there'd been this little flicker of hope that maybe, after everything they'd been through together at the hospital, Natalie wouldn't think the extravagance of his gift was all that weird. He'd hoped maybe she'd see all the cute airplanes, and the shiny, new furniture, and instead of making her feel uncomfortable, it would make her feel, well, happy.

He really wanted to make Natalie happy.

Instead, though, right now she looked a little crumpled. She wore the expression of a woman who'd just been handed a fresh problem on top of everything else she was dealing with. That wasn't what he'd been shooting for at all.

She caught him looking at her, and she offered him a tense smile that didn't quite reach her eyes. "Well, I'm sure starting to understand why everybody in town owes you favors."

Ethan stirred and made a fussy noise, and

they both turned to look at him. He was squirming in his car seat.

"He's hungry, I think," Natalie said.

"Probably." He stood there for another minute before realization kicked in. She needed privacy. "Oh! Okay. I'll…uh…wait outside."

"Good." She leaned over and began to unfasten the straps around the unhappy baby. "Because you and I need to have a little talk."

Jacob shut the nursery door behind him and headed through the kitchen to the backyard. He'd better go outside and coax Rufus back in his pen now because he had a feeling this conversation with Natalie might take a while. Especially when she saw all the food he'd trucked in from Bailey's and the church's coffee shop.

He felt a prickle of apprehension. Natalie had already made it clear how she felt about him butting in to her business, but now he'd overstepped her boundaries again. She was going to want to know why.

He should probably tell her.

Chapter Seven

As soon as Ethan's tummy was full, he fell asleep again. Natalie laid her baby on the fresh, crisp sheets of the new crib and hung over the rail for a long moment, just watching him. She already loved him so much. In fact, the feeling was so intense and overwhelming that it scared her a little.

This new nursery scared her a little, too, and for some of the same reasons.

Like her sleeping son, it seemed too good to be true. She hadn't allowed herself to daydream much about pretty baby things she couldn't possibly afford, but if she'd dreamed up the perfect nursery for her little boy, it would have looked exactly like this.

And if she'd dreamed up the perfect man, he'd have looked a lot like Pastor Jacob Stone.

And very little like Adam Larkey.

Natalie nibbled on the inside of her bottom lip and gave herself a talking-to. Since she'd come to Pine Valley, Jacob had done more for her than anybody else in her whole life. It was perfectly natural for her to be having some warm, fuzzy feelings, especially since Adam still hadn't replied to her texts.

But it wasn't smart.

It was Jacob's job to help people, and he was obviously good at it. Why else would everybody around her owe him favors? No matter how it made her feel, none of his kindness was particularly personal.

She had to watch her step.

After all, she'd followed her feelings into trouble before. Ethan was proof enough of that. No, you couldn't trust your feelings.

And you sure couldn't assume that when people did nice things, it was because they truly cared about you.

That was another lesson she'd learned the hard way.

When she'd been a little girl, a local church had sent a bus to the housing project on Sunday mornings. There was a free breakfast involved, so several of the children, including Natalie, made sure to be on it.

The pancakes were only part of the attraction, though. The church was warm and clean, and the people were so friendly and didn't seem to mind that the project kids came wearing ragged T-shirts and jeans. Most of all, Natalie had loved the peaceful quiet of the lofty church sanctuary, the smell of the candles and the fresh flowers. Since the other kids weren't nearly as interested in the service as they were in the food, Natalie started slipping away to sit by herself in the corner of a pew where she could concentrate on what the grandfatherly looking minister was saying. Natalie thought he must be the kindest, wisest man in the whole world.

Then one morning, the woman sitting in front of her had fussed to her seatmate about the "trashy housing project children" that the outreach committee insisted on "bussing in."

"The minister doesn't like it any more than we do. In fact, he's stopped his own grandchildren from attending Sunday school because they contracted lice from one of those dirty kids. But he says his hands are tied because taking care of poor people is the duty of the church, whether we want them here or not."

Natalie had climbed back on the project bus that afternoon with a lowered head and stinging cheeks. It had taken ten years and an unexpected pregnancy to get her under the roof of a church again.

As it turned out, she should have learned her

lesson the first time. And she certainly couldn't afford to forget it now.

There was way too much at stake.

When she came in the kitchen, Jacob was sitting at the table, scrolling through messages on his phone. He rose to his feet and slipped the device into his pocket.

"Well, I put Rufus back in. No telling how long he'll stay there, though. Here." He retrieved a glass of milk from the refrigerator, placing it on the table alongside a plate containing red grapes and a big wedge of cheese. "The nurses said you should eat lots of calcium. I'm not much of a cook, but I do snacks like a boss." He pulled out a chair. "Have a seat."

He'd softened the wooden seat with a plump red cushion. A yellow price tag still dangled from one corner.

Her heart melted, but she had to stick to her guns. "I need to talk to you, Jacob."

"You can talk sitting down." He patted the back of the chair invitingly before settling back into his own.

She hesitated. She felt more in charge of herself standing up. But she also felt awkward and a little unsteady.

She sat.

"Okay." He nudged the plate an inch closer to her. "Let's talk."

Natalie broke off a bit of cheese and put it in her mouth to buy some time. She had no idea how she could say what she had to say without seeming rude.

Jacob broke the silence. "Look, I know I blindsided you with the porch and the nursery. I guess I owe you an explanation. I really don't want you to misunderstand why—"

Oh no. She felt her cheeks heating up. Had she been that obvious? She'd thought she'd kept those ridiculous flutters well hidden. "That's okay," she interrupted him. "I know this isn't personal. I'm sorry if I've seemed too emotional about…everything."

She darted an embarrassed glance at him. He was frowning at her. "I'm not sure what you mean. And this may not be personal for you, but it's pretty personal for me. That's what I'm trying to tell you."

Natalie hadn't known that a person could be so hot and so cold at the same time. Her cheeks were burning, but her arms had goose bumps.

What did he mean this was *personal*?

"I never planned to be a minister." He cleared his throat. "Back in college I had my sights set on being a football star. I always tell people that God had to tackle me to get my attention, and He used a linebacker from Miami to do it." A smile flickered briefly. "Blew out my knee. It was my junior year of college. I argued with God for two more years, but He won out in the end. I was twenty-two when I became a Christian." He paused, lifted his chin and looked her straight in the eye. "My daughter was born when I was nineteen."

The old refrigerator chugged loudly behind him, and static crackled from the baby monitor she'd placed on the table, but the kitchen seemed suddenly very quiet. Jacob held her stunned gaze with his.

"You have a daughter?"

"Yes. And no." He hesitated, then laughed shortly. "Wow, I haven't told this story in a long time. It's harder than I thought."

"It's okay." So that was why he'd never acted judgmental about her predicament. Because he'd been through this, too. Impulsively, Natalie reached across the table and covered his hand lightly with her own. "Take your time."

"My girlfriend…her name was Carrie…found out she was pregnant during our freshman year in college. Like I said, I wasn't a believer back then, and neither was she. We were both really young. We talked about a lot of options, but in the end, we gave the baby up for adoption the day she was born."

"Oh." Natalie released his hand and sat back in her chair. "Do you see her?"

"No. It's a closed adoption. At the time, we both thought that was the best idea. Now I think it would've been better if there was some way I could have…been there for my little girl if she ever needed me. So if I've been a little pushy about helping you and Ethan while Adam's away, that's why. Because I hope that somewhere, some other guy is being there for my daughter. I hope you can understand."

Natalie nodded slowly. "I think I do."

"I guess it's normal to wonder, you know? What kind of life she has now, if she's happy. Things like that."

He looked so wistful that her resolve wavered. She tried to imagine what she'd feel like if Ethan was with another family, and she didn't know anything about him.

Awful. It would feel awful.

"You could check with the adoption agency." When he looked at her, she dropped her eyes and studied her fingernails. "When I first found out I was pregnant, I wasn't sure what I was going to do. So I went and talked to an agency in Atlanta. They were really nice, but I decided there was just no way I could…" She stopped and darted a glance at him. "Anyway, they had a deal where the adoptive family sent in updates every year until the child turned eighteen. The birth parents could see those if they wanted to, even if the adoption was closed. Maybe the agency you used does something like that, too."

"I don't know." He sounded interested. "But I can check into it. That's a good idea, Natalie. Thanks. And seriously, thanks for allowing me to butt in to your life. I hope you'll keep on letting me help out, until Adam comes back." He hesitated. "Have you…heard anything from him?"

"Not yet." The little tickle of uncertainty she'd been pushing away popped up front and center. She'd texted Adam several times since Ethan's birth. She'd even sent him pictures of his son, but the only response had been dead silence. "I'm not sure if he's getting the messages."

"He may not be. Lots of things can happen on a hiking trip. His phone could be dead or broken, or he might be in some place without a signal. If that's the problem, he'll contact you when he gets back to civilization."

"Maybe. There's no telling with Adam." She took a deep breath. "I'll just have to manage until he turns back up."

Jacob reached across the table and covered her hand with his. "I'd like to help with that, if you'll still let me. And don't worry." He flashed a boyish grin. "I promise I'll behave from here on out. I won't buy Ethan a pony or a sports car or anything."

Natalie hesitated. This might not be a good idea. Jacob's touch was making her insides flutter a little too much for jumbled hormones to be the only reason.

"I guess that would be all right," she heard herself saying.

"Thanks." This time, the warmth of his smile went right up into his sea-blue eyes. She felt her battered heart flip over and fluff up like a freshly turned pancake.

No, she realized, just a few seconds too late. Spending more time with Jacob Stone was definitely not a good idea.

Chapter Eight

A week and a half later, at exactly 6:45 a.m., Jacob was on the back porch of the Lark Hill farmhouse having a standoff with a goat. Rufus had his two front hooves on the bottom step and a hopeful expression on his face.

"You know you're not allowed in the house, Rufus. Shoo. Go back to your pen."

The goat snorted at him and tossed his head, flopping his curly topknot. The animal made a quick move to the right, but Jacob blocked him.

"Nope." The animal tilted his head winningly and batted his eyes. "Nice try, but still no. Ethan's about to go back to sleep, and you're staying outside. In your pen."

The goat made a disgusted noise. He eyed his opponent thoughtfully for a second or two, then attempted a death-or-glory charge up the steps. Jacob snagged him by the collar just as he reached the screened door.

"Gotcha!" He manhandled the protesting goat back down the steps and led him in the direction of his pen.

He and Rufus had tussled several times, but lately the animal was making even more of a nuisance of himself than usual. When Jacob had arrived at Lark Hill fifteen minutes ago, he'd found the goat on the back porch, nibbling on the doorknob.

Deep down, Jacob felt a sneaking sympathy for the old rascal. After all, he was doing pretty much the same thing himself. The only difference was, Natalie actually allowed him in the house.

So far, anyway. He worried he was on the brink of wearing out his welcome, but he just couldn't seem to stay away.

He'd arrived this morning around six thirty, the earliest time he'd clocked in yet. To make matters worse, he hadn't left last night until nearly 10:00 p.m. But he couldn't help that; Natalie's clothes dryer had been acting up, and it had taken him that long to figure out how to fix it.

Of course, repairing the dryer probably could have waited, and taking the thing apart at eight thirty last night hadn't been the best idea. But when Natalie had turned it on, and he'd heard the rattle, he'd overridden her protests and hauled his tools in from his truck. He'd heard of malfunctioning dryers causing house fires, and he wanted to make sure the old appliance was safe.

He'd also been glad for the excuse to hang around Lark Hill a little longer. He didn't like leaving Natalie and Ethan out here alone at night, especially since her car wasn't ready yet. Mike had needed to order a part, and though the mechanic had been apologetic about the delay, there'd been no way around it.

Besides, Jacob liked tinkering around the old farmhouse, hearing snatches of whatever song Natalie happened to be humming at the moment and the little baby noises Ethan had started to make. He liked shouldering through the kitchen doorway with his arms full of grocery bags, seeing Natalie's face light up at the little treats he brought her, something she only allowed because more often than not, he just happened to be hanging around Lark Hill at suppertime.

That wasn't quite as accidental as he made it seem.

The truth was, he loved sitting at the old kitchen table as it slowly grew dark outside. He'd jam a knee against its wonky leg so it wouldn't wobble too much and nestle Ethan in the crook of his arm, insisting that Natalie eat the simple meal she'd prepared while it was still hot. Natalie fretted about Jacob's food going cold, but he honestly couldn't have cared less if it did.

He wasn't eating alone. That was all that mattered to him.

These evenings were welcome bits of peace for him, given that the church situation had only gotten worse. In spite of his prayers for guidance, God seemed to have him in some kind of holding pattern. So for now, he was fidgeting through Digby's endless meetings, cringing as the fellowship hall plans grew more and more grandiose and further out of step with his own convictions.

He'd have exploded by now if he hadn't had these evenings with Natalie and Ethan to look forward to. He knew it was wrong to be glad that Adam still hadn't turned up, but he couldn't help it.

In fact, the one and only thing he didn't much like about this arrangement he had with Natalie was that it could end at any moment.

But it hadn't ended yet, and right now he had a goat to deal with.

Jacob shut Rufus in his shed and walked out to inspect the fence. He'd have to figure out where the goat had escaped this time and fix it. Not that it would do much good. Rufus was living up to his reputation, and the animal spent more time outside his pen than in it.

Jacob glanced at his watch. If he started working on the fence now, he'd have to go home and clean up afterward. That meant he'd be late getting to the church. Still, Rufus couldn't stay shut up in his shed for very long, and he sure couldn't run loose all day. He'd aggravate Natalie to death.

Jacob headed toward his truck, fishing his cell phone out of his pocket. He'd fix the pen and be late. He'd better let Arlene know.

His secretary picked up on the second ring and didn't wait for him to speak. "I know, I know. You're going to be late. Again."

"Not very."

Arlene's sigh gusted through the phone so loudly he could almost smell her wintergreen breath mints. "This is the third time you've run late this week, and you've left early twice. This isn't like you, Jacob. You're worrying me."

"Relax. I'll make Digby's ten o'clock meeting with the architect." The third architect they'd talked to. So far. And from the look of his embossed business card, the most expensive one yet.

"I'm not worried about Digby! I could cheerfully strangle that man. Him and his horrible meetings! He's the reason you've gone all squir-relly. I just know it. Now, you tell me the truth. Have you decided to resign? Are you going to job interviews? Is that why you're out of the of-fice so much?"

His secretary's voice quavered a little on the question, and Jacob felt a twinge of regret. Ar-lene might be crusty and outspoken, but she was also a faithful friend and coworker.

He owed her the truth.

"I'm not going to job interviews."

"Thank goodness."

"Not yet, anyway, and I hope it won't come to that. I'm still praying about it."

"So am I, believe me." Arlene sounded grim. "But if you're not out looking for another job, then where *are* you spending all your time?"

Jacob reached for the metal box of tools he kept stashed in the cab of his truck. "I'll see you at ten, Arlene."

"So, it's true, then." Something in Arlene's tone snapped Jacob to attention. Unfortunately, he *hadn't* snapped the latches on the toolbox after working on the dryer, and it opened, spill-ing its contents in, around and under the truck.

Great.

"I don't know what you're talking about, and I'm kind of busy right now, Arlene."

"You're out there helping that Good Shepherd

bride, aren't you? I've been hearing some talk, but you hadn't said anything, so I thought it was just gossip. This isn't good, Jacob. If Digby finds out…"

"What I do with my personal time is none of Digby's business."

"He's not going to see it that way, and you know it."

"Natalie had nobody to turn to, Arlene, and she needed help. Any church that won't step up in a situation like that has something seriously wrong with it." He knelt down and peered beneath the truck. Two screwdrivers had rolled so far under there that he was going to have to lie flat on the ground to reach them.

Good thing he was already planning to change clothes.

"But the church didn't step up, did it? *You* did." Arlene paused. "You took all that time off work, and you've been so preoccupied lately. I thought you must have some kind of digestion problem from those dreadful microwave burritos you're so fond of, but now… Jacob, tell me the truth. How *personal* is this personal time you've been taking, exactly?"

Jacob clenched his phone between his cheek and his shoulder, inching his fingers across the damp grass toward the runaway tools. "I'm not romantically involved with Natalie Davis, if that's what you're asking me."

But I'd like to be.

The thought came out of nowhere, along with a flood of longing that slammed him squarely in his gut. The feeling was so sharp and so painful that he jerked upward, banging his head hard against the underside of the truck cab.

Abandoning the screwdrivers, he slid out from under the vehicle and sat up slowly, rubbing his head. He was stunned in a way that had nothing to do with the blow he'd just taken. He reached for the phone he'd dropped and held it back to his ear.

Arlene was still talking. "...why you hadn't brought her to church, but of course, with her just getting over having the baby and all, I suppose it makes sense. But you really do need to watch your step, Jacob. Digby's nephew—"

Digby's nephew was the last thing he wanted to think about right now. "I'm hanging up, Arlene."

He dropped his phone back into his shirt pocket and rubbed his aching head.

"Are you all right?"

He looked up. Natalie was standing on the back doorstep, dressed in her baggy maternity smock, her face crumpled in concern. She hurried over to where he was sitting dazedly on his heels. Laying her hand lightly on top of his head, she ruffled his hair as she checked his scalp. "That looked like it hurt. Are you bleeding? Do you need some ice?"

The feel of her small hand in his hair wasn't helping with the crazy feelings churning around inside him, but he couldn't seem to move away. "No. I'm fine."

"What were you doing under there, anyway?" Her hand lifted, and the fog in Jacob's brain cleared a little.

"Getting ready to fix Rufus's fence again." He focused on chucking the gathered tools back into the toolbox one by one. "Houdini was on the back steps when I got here. How's Ethan this morning?"

"Asleep." Natalie showed him the baby monitor in her hand. "Finally. He was up a lot last night. Are you sure you have time to do this now? Won't it make you late getting to the church?"

"Not much. I'll just give the latest escape route a quick patch job and head on over there." He hesitated, remembering what Arlene had said just now, about him not giving the church a chance to step in.

Why *hadn't* he invited Natalie to Pine Valley Community? Usually that was the second sentence out of his mouth after he met people.

But with Natalie, he hadn't even brought it up, and he wasn't sure why.

Better late than never, though.

"Speaking of church, I'd really like you to meet the members of my congregation. How about going with me this Sunday?"

"I don't think that would be a good idea." She suddenly seemed to have a lot of trouble meeting his eyes, but she offered him a brief smile.

"It's just… I don't have anything to wear to church." She tugged at the waistband of her maternity pants. "These are too loose now, but all my regular clothes are in boxes I left with a co-worker back in Atlanta. Adam and I were going to pick them up, but…" She left the sentence unfinished. "Right now I'm making do with safety pins, but I wouldn't risk going to your church with pants that could fall down at any moment."

"No, I suppose not." How stupid of him not to have noticed.

Still… As a minister, he'd heard an awful lot of excuses, and there was something about Natalie's explanation that didn't quite ring true.

Natalie glanced back at the farmhouse. She seemed suddenly anxious to get away from him. "Ethan will be up before long. I think I'll go inside and try to get a nap. And please don't make yourself late on Rufus's account. No matter what we do, he'll be out again in an hour."

She gave him another quick smile and hurried back toward the house. She kept one hand on her sagging waistband, but Jacob still wasn't convinced that her oversize clothes were the real reason she'd refused his invitation.

Fortunately, there was an easy way to find out. He'd take care of that the first chance he got.

As he watched Natalie go, a bluebird flittered down to perch on one of Rufus's leaning fence posts and burst into a wildly happy song. As Jacob listened, he was suddenly aware of the warmth of the morning sun on his shoulders and the springy young grass under his feet.

Well, what did you know? Spring had finally bloomed in Pine Valley, and he hadn't even realized it.

Until now.

"Togs?" Natalie read the script on the big bag Jacob had just set on the kitchen table. She was standing at the sink trying to finish washing up her breakfast dishes while Ethan squirmed and fussed in his bouncy seat. "What's that?"

"According to all the women in town, the only clothing store in Pine Valley worth shopping in. You'd better try everything on. I didn't know your size, so I had to wing it. I saved the receipt, so if they don't fit, we can swap them."

Natalie stared, her dishcloth dripping into the sudsy water. "You bought me clothes?"

"Don't worry. I didn't pick them out. The lady who owns the store chose them."

"Jacob." Natalie wrung out the cloth and draped it over the faucet, searching for the right words. "Helping out around here is one thing. Buying me clothes…"

"I know," he interrupted. "It's too personal and inappropriate and all that stuff. But you're losing weight fast, and you need something that fits. And I really didn't buy much this time, just the basics. Here." He nudged the bag in her direction. "See for yourself."

Natalie hesitated, but curiosity won out. She peeked into the sack while Jacob unfastened Ethan from his padded seat and settled the unhappy infant against his shoulder.

"Marla called those stretchy pants leggings," he said when she set two pairs on the table. "I don't know anything about women's clothes, but they looked comfortable. There are some shirts to match. And a pair of jeans."

Natalie drew out two flowing button-up shirts. "This is really thoughtful of you." She stroked a silky shirt with one finger. It was patterned all over with blurry-looking pastel flowers, and it looked feminine and delicate. She'd never owned anything so pretty in her life.

"Do you think they'll fit?"

Natalie slipped her fingers into the collar to check on the size. She tried a discreet check of the price tag too, but Jacob had torn off the part that told the cost.

Not that it mattered. She couldn't possibly have afforded them anyway, and after the nursery, she'd made up her mind that she wasn't allowing Jacob to give her anything else. He meant well, but accepting charity always ended up causing trouble. The last thing she needed right now was more of that.

Besides, the man's own shirt collar was frayed at the edges. If he had any spare money, he ought to be spending it on things for himself.

She piled the pretty clothes back into the bag and pushed it in his direction. "This was very sweet of you, Jacob, but you'll have to take them back. I already told you. I'm not accepting any more gifts."

He didn't look happy, but he nodded. "Okay, if you insist. We'll consider it a loan. Here." He rummaged in his pocket and pulled out a crumpled receipt. "This is what I spent. You can pay me back when you're able."

She hesitated a second before reaching for the paper. She smoothed it out and scanned the total, frowning. "This doesn't seem like very much for such nice clothes."

"Yes, well, Marla gave me a discount."

"Why would she do that?" Natalie's heart sank. Probably because Jacob had mentioned the outfits were for somebody "less fortunate." She'd always hated that term, but church people sure were fond of it.

"Because she owed me a favor." He patted Ethan's round bottom soothingly as he smiled at her. "Besides, she likes me."

Natalie chewed on her lower lip thoughtfully. Well. That she could believe. Jacob sure seemed to specialize in doing favors for everybody he knew.

And of course the woman liked him. What woman wouldn't?

Look at him now. He had Ethan cradled expertly against one shoulder, the baby's round head tucked under his chin, patting the little diapered rump patiently. He was also swaying back and forth and making a little humming noise under his breath. His hair was tousled, and there was a wet patch of baby drool expanding on his worn shirt at an alarming rate.

He looked kind of silly.

But to a tired mother who'd been jouncing a fussy baby in her aching arms all morning, he also looked pretty wonderful.

He smiled at her hopefully, and her heart softened. "You're impossible to argue with," she informed him. "You know that, right?"

His grin widened. "That's what everybody tells me."

"Well, okay. It's just a loan, though. I'm paying you back as soon as I possibly can." She pulled the bag back across the table and began unpacking it again. "I have to say, it'll be a big relief to have some pants that actually fit." She unfolded the final item and discovered a dress in a dark rose color. It was loose enough for her to wear comfortably, but it had an elegant simplicity to it. She shot a suspicious look at Jacob.

"A dress? I thought you said you just bought the basics."

"I did. You'll need that for church on Sunday. Of course, you could wear those legging things if they're more comfortable. There's no dress code at Pine Valley Community, and people wear all kinds of clothes."

So that's what this was about. She should have known.

Natalie put the dress back into the bag and shook her head. "Thanks, but I don't think that me going to your church would be a good idea."

Jacob pulled out a chair one-handed and lowered himself slowly into it. Ethan was almost asleep. "I know you're a believer. So, why not?"

Natalie made a short, harsh noise that had Ethan's eyelashes fluttering. "I don't think I need to spell it out for you."

"I think maybe you do."

"Because of my situation."

"What situation is that? Being a single mother? I hate to break it to you, Natalie, but you're definitely not the first woman in our congregation to find herself in that position."

She didn't know quite what to do with that answer, so she changed tactics.

"It's not only that. There's the whole money thing. I need to get back on my feet financially before I—"

"We don't charge admission, Natalie. And anyway, it's the same deal. Half the town's out of work right now, so you'll find plenty of people who understand what you're going through. Come on, it's Mother's Day this Sunday. Your very first one. You wouldn't want to miss that."

"I might."

"And if you're planning to stay here, you'll want to make some friends in the community. No better place to do that than a church."

That's what he thought.

Natalie fidgeted with the sleeve of one of the shirts, wondering how much she should tell him. "The truth is, I don't exactly have the most… heartwarming memories of churches."

"All the more reason to make new ones."

Natalie made a skeptical noise, picked up her dishcloth and busied herself wiping the clean countertop. She could feel Jacob studying her, but he said nothing. Finally, she turned and met his gaze. "Besides, even if I did want to go, I couldn't. Ethan's only a few weeks old. I don't feel comfortable leaving him in a church nursery."

"You won't have to. Don't worry about Ethan. I'll take care of everything."

The man had an answer for everything. "I'm not only worried about Ethan. Or myself. Church people…well, you know what they can be like. I wouldn't want to…cause trouble."

"You couldn't possibly cause any trouble, Natalie."

"Don't be so sure." He kept looking at her, one eyebrow lifted, obviously expecting her to explain. She sighed. "Right after Adam left, when I…turned back to God, I tried going to church. It was nice…for a while." She swallowed and looked down at her hands. "I was so thankful. Those services were my lifeline, you know? They kept me going through some pretty hard days. And then one Sunday, the minister took me aside and told me about this after-school ministry they were doing for kids from the housing projects."

Jacob's eyes lit up. "That sounds like a great outreach!"

"It really was. But some of the workers were having a pretty hard time. They'd never run into kids like the ones who came, you know, kids from the projects. But I had, and he thought maybe I could help make the program better. So I got my manager to rearrange my schedule so I could be at the church every weekday afternoon."

"That was kind of him."

Natalie laughed. "Not really. He made me work the night shift to make up for it, but I didn't mind. I felt like I was really making a difference. For a few weeks, anyway."

"What happened, Natalie?"

"I started to show. Not long after I started wearing maternity clothes, the lady in charge pulled me aside and told me not to come back anymore. She said I was a bad example to the children. She suggested I volunteer to fix plates for the shut-in ministry instead because nobody would see me in the kitchen."

Jacob made a sharp, disapproving noise, causing Ethan to stir against his chest. Jacob soothed him gently, but an angry line remained between his eyebrows. "That's inexcusable. The pastor should have stepped in."

"Oh, he did," Natalie interrupted quickly. "He apologized. He even talked to the program director about it. But the woman's husband was on the board, and they were big contributors to the church, and I was just...*me*. So." She shrugged. "In the end all the minister did was cause a whole lot of trouble for himself." She looked Jacob directly in the eye. "So, are you *sure* you want me to go to church with you?"

"I am." Jacob spoke firmly and without hesitation. He stopped patting Ethan long enough to shove the bag with the dress back across the tabletop in her direction. "No church is perfect, Natalie. That's for sure. But I can tell you this—Pine Valley Community is full of wonderful people with good hearts. They'd love to get to know you and Ethan and welcome you both into the community, the same way they've welcomed me. And remember, I have some personal experience with your kind of situation, myself."

That was true. She hadn't thought about that.

"Do they know? About your daughter, I mean?"

"I didn't put it on my résumé. But I haven't made any secret of it, either. So, yes, a lot of them know. My church is my family, Natalie. I don't hide things from them."

My church is my family. He sure knew the right buttons to push. A family was exactly what she wanted for Ethan. And for herself.

He was still waiting for her answer. Natalie drew in a deep, slow breath and nodded slowly. "All right. I'll go."

Jacob's smile lit up the kitchen. "Great! I'm telling you, you're going to love Pine Valley Community, Natalie."

She hoped he was right. But if he wasn't, if this worked out the way she feared it would, at least he couldn't say she hadn't warned him.

Chapter Nine

The following Sunday morning, Natalie sat in the front pew of Pine Valley Community Church, trying not to fidget. She wished Jacob hadn't insisted that she sit all the way up here. All through the service, she could feel the eyes of his curious congregation boring into the back of her head.

But when she'd protested his choice of seating, he'd dug in his heels, joking that he was putting her up front so she couldn't slip out of the service to check on Ethan.

Proving what she already knew. Jacob Stone was one smart man. If she'd been sitting in the back pew, she'd have sneaked out before the offertory. This first hour away from her baby seemed endless.

It wasn't that Jacob wasn't a good preacher. He was. His Mother's Day topic was "Following

Blind," and it was about the necessity to follow God as unquestioningly as a mother expected her child to follow her. He was really making her think about how fully she was trusting God in her current situation. She'd even found herself using the pencil in the little holder in front of her to make some notes on the back of the bulletin.

His delivery was every bit as good as his subject. Jacob had a casual, friendly style, giving the impression that he was talking personally to each listener.

At least that was the way Natalie had felt. Of course, maybe that was because he seemed to glance in her direction a lot. He'd even grinned down at her once during a hymn when he'd caught her sneaking a peek at her watch. In that second, he'd transformed back from Pastor Stone into Jacob, the guy who'd insisted on rolling up his shirtsleeves to change Ethan's diaper just before the service.

Maybe it was the confusing intimacy she shared with this man, or maybe it was just her wacky postpartum hormones, but her emotions were sure all over the place today.

She'd been really nervous when they'd pulled up in front of this little church today. But so far, things had gone all right. The people she'd spoken to had seemed a little surprised when

Jacob introduced her, but they'd shaken her hand warmly and made her feel welcome.

She'd have felt a little less conspicuous in a different seat, but still, it was a nice change to worship with other people, instead of watching a service on television. When she caught herself checking the back of the bulletin to see what the sermon was going to be about next Sunday, she had to laugh a little.

She hadn't even left yet, and she was already looking forward to coming back.

The minute Jacob had given the benediction, he bounded down the carpeted steps. "Congratulations! You made it through the whole hour."

"I did." She couldn't help but smile back at him. "And it wasn't as hard as I thought it would be. You're a wonderful speaker, Jacob—you really are."

"Thanks." He winked. "As much as I'd love to hog all the credit for that, the truth is, I've got some pretty good material to work with." He held up his worn black Bible, and she laughed. He grinned back, and as he did, his eyes met hers, just the way they'd done countless times before. But this time…

Something felt different.

This time, his gaze looked deeper somehow, and a feminine instinct buried in Natalie's heart woke up.

Jacob Stone had looked at her hundreds of times, sure. But never like this. Right now in the front of this church—she didn't know how to explain it, even to herself, but it was as if he was really *looking*.

At *her*.

She suddenly found it hard to draw a deep breath. He reached out, his hand closing gently over her upper arm. She jumped like a startled deer, but he didn't seem to notice.

"Look, Natalie, I've got to say goodbye to everybody. You go pick up Ethan and meet me at the front door in a few minutes, okay? This part can take a while, so if you need to feed him, just lock my office door and take your time. We're in no hurry."

He gave her arm a little squeeze and started down the center aisle of the church, shouldering his way through his congregation. The murmuring in the sanctuary hushed as the people paused for a second or two, watching Jacob thread his way toward the door.

Natalie saw people shooting some curious glances at her, too, but for once she didn't really care. She stood frozen where Jacob had left her, trying to collect her thoughts.

That—whatever it was—had to have been her imagination. To think anything else was just ridiculous.

Wasn't it?

She suddenly noticed a gaggle of older women heading in her direction with determined looks on their faces, and her heart skipped nervously. She'd enjoyed the service, but church ladies were her personal kryptonite, and she definitely wasn't feeling up to coping with them right now. She slipped up the side aisle and escaped just in time.

Once safely out of the sanctuary, Natalie hurried down the carpeted hallway toward Jacob's office. That's where she'd left Ethan with Beth Pruitt.

A grandmotherly lady with a kind face, Mrs. Pruitt had been Jacob's answer to Natalie's refusal to leave her tiny two-week-old baby in the church nursery.

"She can look after him right here," Jacob had assured her. "Ethan will be just fine. Mrs. Pruitt is the most experienced baby spoiler in town."

"Don't you worry, dearie," Mrs. Pruitt had said, reaching for Ethan with a gentle smile. "Go have yourself some good fellowship time with the Lord. I'll sit right here in this chair and rock your sweet little boy for you."

"I hate for you to miss the Mother's Day service on my account," Natalie had hedged, hovering nervously as the old lady settled herself and Ethan into the creaking chair.

"Oh, I won't miss a thing." She'd patted a square black box on the table beside her. "Pastor Jacob takes better care of me than that. This gizmo right here broadcasts the whole service." She lifted up an earbud with one gnarled finger. "I slip this little thingamabob in my ear, and I can turn it up as loud as I want. Now get on with you, and like I said, don't you worry a bit. I'm an old hand at babies. Had six of my own, then I was blessed with ten grandchildren. I've already lost count of my great-grands."

There wasn't any reasonable argument she could make in the face of that kind of maternal experience. Natalie had glanced up into Jacob's face and caught a glimmer of triumphant amusement lurking in his eyes. She'd been outmaneuvered.

She paused outside a closed door with a sign reading Pastor's Office. She liked how everything in this building seemed to be neatly labeled, making it easier for a newcomer to find her way around. She opened the door and sure enough, there was the church secretary's prim desk with its neatly aligned stacks of folders.

The door to Jacob's private office was shut. Natalie crossed the small room and hesitated. Should she knock? Probably not. Then Mrs. Pruitt would just have to get up out of the chair to open the door. Better to just go on in. As Natalie put her hand on the doorknob, she heard the elderly babysitter's wavering voice.

"Calm down, Arlene. You'll wake the baby."

"How can I calm down?" a sharper voice demanded. "I'm telling you, this is a complete disaster."

"Well now, I don't see why everybody has their feathers so ruffled. She seems perfectly sweet to me, and this little fellow is just precious. I think it's lovely that Pastor Jacob has finally found himself somebody special to dote on."

"He's not *doting* on her. It's not like that at all! I have it straight from Jacob's own lips that there's nothing romantic going on. This whole thing is nothing but another one of his Good Samaritan projects. If a church won't step up in a situation like that, what good is it? Those are almost his exact words. I know he wants to make a point with the church board about the foolishness of building the fellowship hall right now. You know, pointing out the needy folks around us, and all of that. But taking that girl down to the pastor's family pew, in front of everybody? He might as well have spit in Digby Markham's face. It's asking for trouble, that's what, and more trouble's the last thing we need right now. I could just wring his neck."

Suddenly, the brass doorknob turned under

Natalie's hand. She had just enough time to step back before the door swung open.

A tall iron-haired lady with vivid fuchsia lipstick paused awkwardly on the threshold. "Ah. Hello. You must be…"

"Natalie Davis." Her voice sounded strained, but at least she managed to keep it from shaking. "I'm here to get my baby."

"He's right here, the little darling." Beth Pruitt smiled from her chair, but she darted worried glances between Natalie and Arlene. "He didn't make a peep the whole time. Slept right through."

Natalie edged past Arlene into the office. Ethan seemed blissfully unaware of the tension in the small room, but Natalie felt an overwhelming urge to snatch him up and run.

"Excuse me, ma'am. Are you Miss Davis?" A male voice spoke behind her. She turned with Ethan in her arms to see a man standing in the doorway. "The preacher said I'd find you in here. I'm Mike. I own the garage in town, and I wanted to let you know that your car's ready. Pastor Jacob said you needed it just as soon as it was safe to drive so I've patched it together as best I can. But I have to be honest with you, you'd probably better start shopping around for a new one. This one's on its last legs. I can drive you over to the garage to pick it up now, unless—" he paused, glancing at the three women "—you have something you need to finish up in here."

"No," Natalie assured him, feeling Arlene's gaze on her. "I'm all done here."

That might just be the understatement of the century.

She turned to Beth Pruitt. "Thanks for watching Ethan."

The old lady looked troubled. "Aw, honey, you're more than welcome. I'll be here next Sunday, ready to rock that sweet boy again, if you'd like."

Natalie smiled politely, but she didn't answer. She already knew she wouldn't be back at this church next Sunday.

Or any other Sunday for that matter.

Carrying her baby, she edged past Arlene through the doorway. Arlene cleared her throat as if she were about to say something, but Natalie quickly averted her eyes and hurried down the hall after Mike.

Jacob was standing in the arched doorway of the church, smiling and shaking hands with a winding line of church members. Mike sidled through the people waiting in line, and Natalie followed him, murmuring apologies to the people she brushed against. Her cheeks felt like they were on fire, and she was careful not to look in Jacob's direction.

She should never have come. She'd known better. But Jacob had been so persuasive...

Maybe because Arlene was right. Because he wanted to use her to prove some kind of point to his congregation.

"Natalie? How'd Ethan do? Did Mike tell you about the car?" She winced as Jacob spoke from the head of the line, pitching his voice to carry over the babble of voices. The murmuring died down instantly, and the little foyer of the church was hushed and expectant as curious heads swiveled in her direction.

Natalie forced herself to smile. "Ethan did fine, Pastor Stone. Thanks for arranging the sitter for me. Mike and I are going to pick my car up right now, so you won't need to give us a ride back home."

She caught a quick glimpse of the surprise clouding Jacob's expression as she slipped past him and out into the parking lot.

Mike was already in the process of transferring Ethan's car seat from Jacob's truck into his own. Natalie stood on the sidewalk, her artificial smile painfully in place, watching him wrestle with the contraption.

Hurry up. Please hurry up. She needed to

get out of here before Jacob could tear himself away from his congregation and come after her.

A picture of him flashed through her mind, his face alight in an easy grin, dimples denting in his cheeks, golden hair all tousled because he was forever running his hands through it. There was the way he'd opened doors for her and steadied her arm when they walked together. And the way he'd looked at her just now in this beautiful church. Her stomach constricted into a quivering knot.

None of that meant anything.

How on earth could she have been so stupid? Had she learned nothing from the mess she'd gotten herself into with Adam?

But no, she'd done it again. Ignored all the warning signs and followed her silly hopes right into trouble.

Well, she'd remember the lessons this time. She wouldn't give up on God. She couldn't. She needed her faith now more than ever. But church, well, church obviously wasn't for her.

And neither was Jacob.

Mike snapped the car seat into his own truck in the nick of time. Natalie gently arranged the straps over her sleepy baby. She climbed in beside Ethan, just as Jacob detached himself from the crowd and walked out into the parking lot.

She could see him in the side mirror of the

mechanic's truck. Seemingly unaware of the whispering crowd behind him, he pulled out his cell phone. Quickly, Natalie took her own out of her purse and powered it down. As Mike turned his truck onto the street, Natalie watched Jacob slide out of the mirror's reflection.

Then she deliberately turned her gaze to the road ahead.

She was beautiful.

Jacob studied the picture of the little girl on his computer screen. He'd been sitting here for the past hour scrolling repeatedly through the five photos the adoption agency had emailed him.

She had Carrie's dark hair, but her eyes were blue like his. She'd also inherited his dimples, which was easy to see because she was smiling in every single picture.

After he'd gotten past the emotional jolt of seeing his daughter's face for the first time, he had scrutinized the background of the photos, searching for clues about her life.

He saw a well-kept lawn and a big, goofy dog. The comfortable-looking house had just the right amount of child-friendly disorder. He caught glimpses of artwork posted on a refrigerator and a plump backpack with initials embroidered in pink thread. *EML.*

The pictures gave tantalizing hints but left him with some unanswered questions. Where exactly was she living? How did she do in school? Did she hate math as much as he had? What name did those initials stand for?

He pushed aside the pain of not knowing all the answers. He knew the most important one.

His daughter was doing just fine without him.

That should have made him feel better. And it did. Sort of. But a shadow of sadness dogged his relief.

This little girl was obviously happy, healthy and loved. She had a wonderful life.

He just wasn't a part of it.

He remembered praying the night Carrie had told him about her pregnancy. It was the first prayer he'd prayed since before he'd hit puberty, and he'd fumbled it badly. But the gist of it had been solid enough. *I know we messed up. Help us fix it. And if somebody has to get hurt here, if somebody has to take the hit for this, please let it be me, God. Not Carrie. Not the baby. Me.*

He didn't doubt that God had heard him. That long night had begun the slow turn back to the faith his parents had tried to instill in him, a change that had gone deeper and further than a guilt-stricken college quarterback could ever have imagined.

In the end, God had worked all things for good, just as He promised to do.

His little girl had a good family. Last he'd heard, Carrie was happily married and moving on with her life. And he'd found more purpose in his calling as a minister than he ever would have playing professional football.

But right now, sitting alone here at his cluttered desk, wondering what his daughter's favorite food was, or what color she liked best, or what her *name* was, for crying out loud, Jacob was taking the hit.

The phone rang, distracting him from his thoughts. He glanced at the screen, hoping it was Natalie. It wasn't. Why was Bailey Quinn calling him in the middle of a busy Monday morning?

Thirty seconds later, he leaned back in his office chair, frowning at the overcrowded bookshelf that Arlene was always nagging him to straighten up. "Natalie did what?"

"Asked me about selling some of her produce here." Bailey's answer came clearly through the line. "She came in first thing this morning, baby in tow."

Natalie must have reached some sort of decision yesterday after she'd left church with Mike to pick up her car. They'd only had one brief conversation since. He'd called her, but she hadn't seemed to want to talk. She'd told him she was planning to run some errands in town this morning and wouldn't be at home, so he shouldn't stop by.

Now he almost wished he hadn't badgered Mike so much about getting those repairs done.

"What's she planning to sell? There's nothing out at Lark Hill except for Rufus, and nobody in his right mind would give her a nickel for him."

Bailey's chuckle rippled in his ear. "I sure wouldn't. No, I'm buying some of her blueberries. We worked it all out."

"Blueberries?" He searched his memory. "What blueberries?"

Bailey sighed. "All the time you've been spending out there, and you didn't notice? Lark Hill's lousy with blueberries, and not just any old blueberries either, city boy. Edgar Larkey spent a mint on those heirloom bushes in the back field, but they've been going to waste ever since he died. They're an early variety, so they're just about to ripen. I've put in a standing order."

"I see." Jacob frowned. He wasn't as much of a city boy as Bailey imagined. He'd picked his share of berries as a kid, and it was slow, tedious work. He didn't see how Natalie could possibly manage to pick the volume of berries

Bailey would want, and he didn't much like the idea of her trying.

"Natalie also asked me about working here part-time. I'm pretty much a one-woman operation at this point, so I sent her over to the church coffee shop. Now that Emily's expecting, I figured Grounds of Faith might be looking for some temporary help."

"You're probably right about that." Although what Natalie would do with Ethan while she did all this was a good question. Blueberry picking, waitressing and taking care of a brand-new baby, too? What on earth was she thinking?

"Anyway, I thought I'd give you a heads-up. I figured you'd want to know, given how…involved you've been with her situation."

"Thanks." Jacob frowned. Bailey seemed to be picking her words carefully. That was unusual.

"And Jacob? Natalie also mentioned something about leaving Pine Valley."

Leaving. His heart thumped hard in his chest. That did it. He and Natalie needed to talk, the sooner the better.

"Thanks, Bailey."

"What was that all about?" Arlene spoke from the doorway just as Jacob ended the call.

Arlene's eavesdropping habit was something they'd discussed more than once, but he didn't have time to reopen that touchy subject right now. He wanted to catch Natalie at Grounds of Faith.

"Coffee shop business," he replied shortly, standing up. "I'm headed there now."

"Does this have something to do with that Davis girl?"

Jacob met Arlene's worried frown head-on. "As a matter of fact, it does. Why?"

"Because, Jacob, you need to be careful. Digby's already gotten his way about the fellowship hall, and there's still his nephew to worry about. Digby would just love to see you out on your ear, and you know it."

"I don't see what all that has to do with Natalie."

Arlene twisted her fingers together, for once apparently at a loss for words. "All I'm saying is that you should let things settle down a bit, that's all. You can help the girl, of course. But you don't need to make such a show of it, not right now, when Digby wants your attention on the fellowship hall plans. If you keep on, you're just going to throw gasoline on this fire, and that's the last thing we need. From what I've heard, Good Shepherd is already gossiping about us. And for once, I'm tempted to agree with them. All this fussing going on in a church is…unseemly."

In spite of everything, the old-fashioned word and the way Arlene's lips pursed up as she said it had Jacob fighting back a grin. Arlene's face had worn the exact same expression once during Vacation Bible School. She'd put her hand in the pocket of little Tommy Anderson's raincoat, expecting to confiscate some smuggled candies. Instead, she'd drawn out an extremely dead lizard.

Apparently, deceased reptiles were *unseemly*, too.

"I'll be back in an hour, Arlene. And I'll bring you back a banana nut muffin and some coffee. Decaf, though. You're too uptight today."

Arlene's frustrated sigh echoed behind him as he headed down the hallway.

Chapter Ten

Normally, Jacob walked the short distance to Grounds of Faith, but he was in a hurry today, so he drove his truck. It was a typical Monday morning, and Pine Valley's downtown square bustled with gentle traffic. Natalie's car was parked just outside the coffee shop's door, and he breathed a prayer of thanks as he pulled in behind it. He hadn't missed her.

The little brass bell on the door jingled cheerily as he entered, and the warm, comforting scents of coffee and cinnamon teased his nose. Grounds of Faith was just finishing up its early-morning rush. About half the tables were filled with customers finishing their coffees, and Jacob noticed that several of them had this week's Bible study leaflet open on their tables. Stacking those by the cash register had been a good idea.

This whole coffee shop ministry had been a good idea. It had met some resistance at first, but now almost everybody had come around. In fact, some of the shop's most outspoken critics were regular customers.

A lot of the credit went to Emily Whitlock. Her arrival in Pine Valley nearly two years ago had been an unmistakable answer to prayer. Her muffins and pastries were nothing short of incredible, and he was grateful that quiet farmer Abel Whitlock had managed to convince Emily to settle down on Goosefeather Farm permanently.

Emily appeared in the open doorway leading to the kitchen area just as he approached the counter. Her face lit up in a welcoming smile, but Jacob's attention zeroed in on Natalie, who was following just behind carrying Ethan.

Natalie was smiling, too, that rare, real smile of hers that warmed her brown eyes. She was wearing one of the outfits he'd given her, and she had her hair pulled up into a loose knot.

For a second, all rational thought left his brain. She looked so sweet standing there with that happy sparkle in her eye and her baby cuddled in her arms.

A jolt of longing hit him. He hadn't seen the two of them since yesterday afternoon, and it had been too long. He'd missed them, both of them.

Natalie's eyes met his. He watched the smile fade from her face, replaced by a wary watchfulness. Jacob's instincts stirred.

Something *was* wrong.

"Hi, Jacob. Making your morning coffee run?" He heard amusement in Emily's voice. She was looking from Natalie's face to his, a smile playing around her lips. "You're a little early, aren't you?"

"Yeah, I'll have my usual, please. Bag up a banana muffin and a cup of coffee for Arlene, too. But she wants decaf today."

"Knowing Arlene, I seriously doubt that, but okay." Emily turned to tug disposable cups out of the dispenser. "I've been getting to know Natalie. She's agreed to help out here for a few weeks. Isn't that great?"

"Bailey mentioned something about that." He kept his eyes focused on Natalie, who was fussing with Ethan's blanket.

"I thought she might have." A laugh lurked somewhere behind Emily's innocent words. Jacob ignored her.

"Natalie, could I speak to you for a minute?"

Natalie glanced up quickly. Before she could respond, Emily reached over and scooped the baby out of his mother's arms.

"You go ahead and talk to Jacob, Natalie. I'll be glad to watch Ethan for a few minutes."

Emily smiled as she looked down at the baby's face. "Good practice for me. It's been a while, and I'll be pulling double duty again in about seven months." She looked back at Jacob, her grin widening. "I was just telling Natalie. The doctor says it's twins again. Abel and I found out at the ultrasound Friday afternoon."

"Congratulations!" His mind flashed back to the pictures on his computer. That longing slammed into him again, this time squarely in the pit of his stomach. "How's Abel handling the news?"

"Just about like you'd expect." Emily's smile deepened and gentled, as it always did when her husband's name was mentioned. "He's been following me around like a shadow, and he won't let me pick up so much as a spoon without trying to help. Paul and Phoebe are arguing over names, and Nana Lois has already broken out her knitting needles. I've got my hands full with the lot of them, believe me. So prayers are much appreciated. Now, go on, have your talk so I can snuggle this baby."

For a second Natalie didn't seem to know what to say. Then her eyes connected with Jacob's, and her doubtful expression firmed up. "Thanks, Emily." She came around the counter and headed toward a corner table. She slid into a chair, clasped her hands on the tabletop and waited until he was seated.

"Mike told me that you paid for the repairs to my car."

It was something about the way she said it. Her voice sounded brittle. Was that what she was upset about? Because he'd settled the mechanic's bill without talking to her about it first?

"I did. I hope that didn't bother you. I know how you feel about me paying for things, Natalie. You can consider it a loan, if you want. I think I have the receipt back at the office."

"Mike already gave me a copy, but thanks. And I'll pay you back, for that and for these clothes, as soon as I can."

"There's no rush."

"I appreciate that." She paused. She seemed to be having a little trouble with what she wanted to say next. "I'm afraid I'm going to have to ask you for one more of those famous favors of yours."

His heart, which had been feeling chilled ever since yesterday, warmed as if some secret switch had been tripped. Natalie, who never asked anybody for anything, was asking him for a favor.

That was a good sign. Wasn't it?

"Sure. Anything. What do you need?"

"I need you to find Adam."

The warm feeling evaporated. "What?"

"I'm sorry to bother you, especially after all you've already done for me. But you have so many connections, and you know just about everybody. I know it's a long shot, but I thought you could put out some feelers and see if you can pin down Adam's location." She straightened her shoulders slightly and set her jaw. "He's still not answering my texts or calls, and I honestly don't know what else to do at this point."

Ask me for anything else, he wanted to tell her. Instead he cleared his throat. "Why now?" He stopped himself. "Sorry. That's none of my business."

Something flickered in her expression, but it was gone before he could put a name to it. "You have the right to know. After all, I'm asking you for help. I want to find out once and for all if he wants to be a part of Ethan's life. If he does…well, I'll do whatever it takes to make that possible."

Whatever it takes. He wasn't sure he liked the sound of that.

"But I need to know. I can't live in this… limbo anymore. I have to make some decisions."

"What kind of decisions?"

"Where I'm going to live for one thing. I can't

stay at Lark Hill if Adam and I aren't getting married. The farm belongs to his family."

"I'm sure I can find you another place in town," he began, but she cut him off.

"I probably won't be staying in Pine Valley. So, do you think you could help me out?"

She wasn't staying. "I'll see what I can do."

"Thank you." She stood and pushed her chair neatly back into place.

She was about to leave. He had to say something. "Rufus," he blurted out. "I…uh…have some new ideas about how to fix his pen. I could drive out later this afternoon and work on it, if that would be all right." She was shaking her head. "Or tomorrow, if that would be more convenient for you."

"Please don't worry about it. I'm going to be kind of busy now, with the new jobs and everything. Besides, Rufus and Ethan and I have already taken up way too much of your time. I'm sure you have some other… Good Samaritan projects you need to be focusing on."

He frowned. That was an odd choice of words. What was going on? "Natalie—" he started, but she cut him off.

"Would you call me, though? As soon as you have any news about Adam, I mean?"

She didn't say *and not before*, but he heard it as plainly as if she had. This was more than just him paying for those repairs. Natalie was shutting him out of her life and slipping away. He desperately didn't want that to happen, but he wasn't sure how to stop it.

"Sure," he said miserably.

"Thanks." She gave him a quick nod, then stole her baby from Emily's arms and said her goodbyes.

He sat at the table for another second or two, listening to the coffee shop bell chiming as the door shut behind her and thinking hard.

That remark she'd just made about charity projects, and the odd way she'd scampered off from church like a spooked deer, calling him *Pastor Stone*. The puzzle pieces slowly clicked into place, and he didn't much like the picture they made.

Somebody at church must have said something to her. He felt a surge of annoyance so strong it bordered on fury, but guilt followed close on its heels. This was his fault. He was the one who'd talked Natalie into going, even insisting that she sit at the very front of the church, in the pew where the members of the pastor's family traditionally sat.

He'd gotten a little carried away. It was just that never once in all the years he'd preached at Pine Valley, had he ever had anybody to put in that pew.

No wonder tongues had started to wag. He might as well have painted a bull's-eye on Natalie's back. She'd already been pretty doubtful about attending services. Now she probably never wanted to darken the door of a church again.

He was an idiot.

He'd have to find out what had happened and see if he could do some damage control. As soon as he got back to the office, he needed to have a little sit-down with Arlene. If anybody could find out what had been said to Natalie, it would be his secretary.

Maybe he should put Arlene on Adam's trail while he was at it. It would serve him right. She'd drag the guy back to Pine Valley by the ear.

Not that it would do much good if she did. It was obvious to Jacob that if Adam really cared about Natalie or Ethan, he'd have never left in the first place. Jacob drummed his fingers on the table, thinking.

Natalie was right. It *was* time to end this limbo she'd been living in.

The little bell jangled again. He glanced up to see Bailey Quinn sauntering in for her mid-morning coffee break. Bailey might be just the woman he needed to talk to right now. He stood up so fast that his chair clattered to the floor.

Emily and Bailey halted in midgreeting to turn and stare at him.

He crossed the space between them in two long strides, his eyes fixed on Bailey's startled face. Before she could speak, he cut right to the chase.

"Don't you have a friend who's a park ranger?"

Bailey blinked. "Yes. Why?"

"I'm going to need his number."

A few days later, Natalie sat in the quiet farmhouse kitchen, a cup of herbal tea and the baby monitor at her elbow, totaling up numbers on a legal pad while Ethan napped in his nursery. When she finished, she leaned back in the wobbly kitchen chair and sighed.

Her plan was doable. Barely. It wasn't going to be easy, considering how tired she was these days. Getting up twice a night to feed Ethan, then caring for a baby all day long, was even more exhausting than working double shifts as a waitress.

Especially now that Jacob wasn't coming by anymore. She hadn't fully realized how much she'd come to depend on him until she'd told him to stay away. And it wasn't just his help that she missed; she missed his companionship.

She missed his smile.

Of course, he still came by the church coffee

shop every morning, but Natalie always found something to do in the kitchen when he showed up. Emily had shot her a few concerned glances, but she hadn't said anything about it.

Emily had been so kind to her. When Natalie had explained her situation, the coffee shop manager had given her hand a friendly squeeze. "I was a single mom, too, and I know how hard it can be. Bring your baby to work with you. We'll manage."

She'd worked two half days already, and so far Emily was right. Which was good, because Natalie needed the small salary from the coffee shop and every cent she could get from the blueberries if she was going to make ends meet.

Natalie stood, clipping the baby monitor to the waistband of her leggings. While Ethan was sleeping, she'd go check up on the berries. She closed the creaky back door and headed across the backyard.

She walked out into the brambly field, squinting at the bushes stretching out in all directions. Most of the berries on the sagging branches were still a pinkish red, but some of them were beginning to turn a dusky blue. She'd have to start picking them soon, and she honestly didn't know where she'd find the energy.

She should be thankful, she reminded herself. She'd prayed for a way to make some money, and God had provided. Not only had Bailey Quinn promised to buy every berry Natalie could deliver, the shop owner had instantly agreed to the price Natalie had set.

And that wasn't all. Natalie hadn't expected Cora to allow her to sell the blueberries, especially since Adam's grandmother had never even responded to the text Natalie sent her announcing Ethan's birth.

But when Natalie had called to ask permission, Cora had immediately agreed.

"I don't see why not. That's honest work, and they'll just go to waste otherwise." The older woman, who'd sounded hoarse and weak, confessed that she'd been ill with the flu. "It's been going around the retirement villa like wildfire. We've had three deaths, and I spent two nights in the hospital myself. I won't be up to seeing my great-grandson any time soon, I'm afraid."

That was just fine with Natalie. The very last thing she needed right now was to catch the flu, and she certainly didn't want Ethan exposed to it.

After she'd hung up, she realized she'd forgotten to ask Cora if she'd heard from Adam. But surely if she had, she'd have let Natalie know.

It was a little strange. Adam's finances had to be getting low. No doubt he'd discovered Natalie's small stash of bills, but even that should have run out by now.

"Blaaah." Natalie jumped at the noise and turned to find Rufus behind her. A branch studded with half-ripened berries hung out of his mouth.

"Bad goat!" She snatched the twig away. Great. She had no idea that goats liked blueberries, but they obviously did. Making Rufus stay in his pen had just been bumped up on her priority list. "Come on, you ornery old rascal. Let's get you back where you belong." She looped her fingers under the goat's faded collar.

As she turned toward the barn, she saw sunlight glinting off a car that was pulling into her driveway. She didn't recognize the car, but she did recognize the tall figure who unfolded herself from the driver's seat. Maybe Rufus did, too, because the animal took one good look, wrenched away from her grip and skittered nervously back in the direction of his pen all by himself.

Arlene.

Natalie fought a desire to crouch behind the berry bushes and hide until Jacob's secretary left. But Ethan was in the house, and he'd be waking up in a few minutes.

She started across the yard, her heart pounding harder with each step. Arlene saw her coming and stopped just shy of the porch, a gift clutched in her hand and a boxy purse swinging from one elbow. She had a determined expression on her face.

"Hello." Natalie offered the greeting as soon as she was within earshot. "Are you looking for me?"

"Yes." The woman's gray curls bobbed as she nodded. "We haven't officially met. I'm Arlene Marvin, the secretary at Pine Valley Community Church. I'd like a word with you." She thrust out the present, neatly wrapped in a glossy blue paper printed with little yellow ducks. "Here. I brought you a baby nail care kit. Most young mothers don't take good care of their newborn's fingernails. You need to keep them clipped good and short. Babies scratch themselves otherwise."

"Thank you." Natalie had no idea what to say next, and she was grateful when the monitor at her hip crackled. "I'm so sorry, but my son is waking up, Mrs. Marvin. I'm going to have to go in."

"It's Miss. I never married. That's all right. I'll come along with you, if you don't mind."

Natalie did mind, but there was nothing she could do about it, short of being rude. As she led the way through the shabby farmhouse, Arlene looked around with interest.

"You know, hardly anybody in Pine Valley has ever been inside this place. Ed Larkey wasn't one for company. Some folks said he only bought this farm to get away from his wife. Not that I blame him. I knew Cora in school, and she always was the bossiest little thing."

Natalie opened the nursery door and gathered Ethan out of his crib. Arlene halted in the doorway, scanning the room with lifted eyebrows. "Well, I must say." She drew in a long breath. "Jacob's certainly been busy."

Natalie could feel her cheeks pinking up as she carried Ethan to the changing table. She kept her eyes down as she fussed with unfastening the snaps on Ethan's onesie. "Pastor Stone has been really kind to us."

"Don't I wish I had a nickel for every time I've heard someone say that! I'd be a wealthy woman." She wandered around the nursery, peering nearsightedly at various items. "Jacob's always doing something for somebody. It's a fine quality for a pastor to have, of course. Our church believes in helping folks. Always has. I want you to know that."

The hairs on the back of Natalie's neck prickled. She had a feeling Arlene was about to zero in on the reason for this little visit.

"I'm afraid you might have reason to think differently. And that's why I'm here." The old woman cleared her throat, and Natalie braced herself. "I came to apologize."

Natalie froze, a pair of blue elastic pants halfway up Ethan's plump legs. Well, that was unexpected. She fumbled for the right thing to say. "You don't… I mean…that's not necessary."

"Jacob says it is, and this time I'm inclined to agree with him. I don't know how much you overheard on Sunday, but I certainly never meant to hurt your feelings or make you feel unwelcome. I've felt real bad about it ever since, especially when Jacob told me how you'd been treated at that other church you went to. I hope you can forgive me."

"There's nothing to forgive," Natalie answered simply. "Like you said, you didn't mean to hurt my feelings. You had no way of knowing I could hear you talking. That was an accident, by the way. I don't usually listen at doors." She finished pulling up the little pants and settled Ethan against her shoulder before turning to face the older woman. Arlene stood in the middle of Ethan's airplane rug, two red spots burning brightly in her thin cheeks.

Natalie wasn't the only person who was finding this conversation uncomfortable.

"Don't worry about it. I completely understand. Voices carry right through that flimsy door. A person can overhear conversations without half trying. I've told Jacob so a dozen times. Anyway, I appreciate you being so nice about it." Arlene shifted her weight from one orthopedic shoe to the other. "Like I told you before, I never married. Too cantankerous for the menfolk, I expect." A very brief smile flickered over the older lady's lips. "So I never had any children of my own. Over the past few years, I've fallen into the habit of fussing over Jacob like a squawky old hen with one chick. The truth is I'm very…fond of that young man, and I'm more than a little worried about him just now, what with Digby and this whole fellowship hall mess that's going on. But then, I'm sure you know all about that."

Hadn't Arlene mentioned something about a fellowship hall when she was talking to Beth Pruitt? But that was the only time Natalie had heard anything about it.

She shook her head. "No, I'm afraid I don't."

She listened uneasily as Arlene explained the troubles Jacob had been dealing with at work. From what his secretary was saying, he was on the brink of losing his job because he wouldn't kowtow to somebody named Digby.

"You know, I'm kind of surprised Jacob hasn't already told you this," Arlene said finally. "What with all the time you two have spent together lately, I'd have thought it would've come up." There was a questioning glint in her steely blue eyes, and she tilted her head as she waited for Natalie's answer.

Natalie lifted her chin and cuddled Ethan a little closer. "Jacob doesn't share his personal problems with me, Miss Marvin. We don't have that kind of relationship. Like you said back at the church, he was just decent enough to help me out when I had nobody else to turn to. That's all."

"I see." Arlene studied her for a thoughtful second then nodded briskly. "Well then, I—"

Before she could finish her sentence, somebody rapped on the nursery door.

Jacob looked in. "I knocked on the front door, but I guess you ladies were too busy talking to hear. Sorry if I startled you." Natalie bit her lip, wondering how much of the conversation he'd overheard. She couldn't tell from his expression.

"That's right. We were talking, not gossiping, so you can save yourself another lecture. It's time for me to get going, anyway." Arlene paused by Natalie's side and gently took Ethan's pudgy hand in her own. The older lady's face softened. "He's a cute little fellow, isn't he?" She cleared her throat. "He's all right for the moment, but those nails grow fast, so be sure to keep an eye. I'm headed on back to the church.

I'm sure there'll be plenty to see about, what with the preacher out gallivanting again."

She brushed by Jacob, who moved politely aside to let her pass. But his eyes never strayed from Natalie's, and his expression remained unreadable.

What was he doing here?

"Abel Whitlock just pulled up in the driveway." Arlene's voice called from the front door.

Natalie shot a questioning look at Jacob. "What's Emily's husband doing all the way out here?"

"I asked Abel to take a look at the goat fence. Maybe he can figure out how to fix it. I hope you don't mind, but Rufus can't run loose all the time. He'll drive you crazy in a week."

"I suppose you're right." Ethan squirmed in her arms and began to fuss. "He just woke up from his nap," Natalie found herself explaining. "He's hungry."

Jacob nodded. "I'll go outside and see what Abel has to say about that pen." There was no trace of his normal, easy smile. He looked so serious that it was making her nervous.

She cleared her throat. "Is…something wrong?"

"Go ahead and feed the baby, Natalie, while

I see what Whitlock thinks about that fence. Then we need to talk." He stepped backward and closed the door.

Laurel Blount 191

Lace when Natalie's thanks about thing fizzy
to lay the good as all... the edges are too warm
and shrub the floor.

Chapter Eleven

"See?" Inside the goat's dilapidated pen, Jacob pulled on the wobbly fence post. "I've fixed this one twice already. He just butts it until it comes loose again. No matter what I do, he gets right back out."

Abel Whitlock nodded, one tanned hand tousling Rufus's topknot. Rufus stared up at him adoringly. Whitlock wasn't much of a talker, but he definitely had a way with animals.

Jacob glanced back at the house. He needed to get this goat situation dealt with. He and Natalie had an important conversation to get through. "So what do you think? Can you fix it?"

Abel scanned the fence and shook his head. "You'd do better to tear this whole thing down and rebuild."

"I was afraid of that."

"Even that might not do you a lick of good."

Abel's mouth quirked up into a lopsided smile. "I expect Rufus here would find a way through any fence we put up. Goats are smart animals, and he's got a stubborn streak a mile wide to boot."

Jacob sighed. "I was really hoping you could help. Natalie has a soft spot for the old rascal."

A troubled look crossed Abel's lean face. "This goat may turn out to be the least of your problems, Stone."

Jacob frowned. "What do you mean?"

"Special church board meeting's been called." Abel shook his head. "I got the email this morning. Still don't know what they were thinking when they asked me to serve on something like that."

Jacob did his best to look innocent. That had been his suggestion, but he wasn't about to admit it. Abel was the only person Jacob knew who hated meetings and committees worse than he did, but Jacob had wanted somebody on the church board with Abel's old-fashioned common sense. "What's the meeting about?"

"You." Abel gave a short nod toward the farmhouse. "And her, I expect. I figure Digby Markham intends to do a little meddling in your personal life. I thought you might appreciate a heads-up."

"I see." A chill settled over Jacob's heart. "Thanks. So when's this meeting?"

"Thursday at four thirty. I'd appreciate it if you'd be there."

"Am I invited?" Sometimes the pastor attended, sometimes he didn't.

"*I'm* inviting you." Stubborn lines creased Abel's tanned forehead. "Never have held with talking behind people's backs. Folks have something to say, they can say it right to your face."

That ought to be fun. Jacob nodded shortly. "All right. I'll be there."

"Digby's bound to come loaded for bear. You'd better do the same."

"Don't worry about me."

"Never do. Not much, anyway." Abel's crooked grin flashed again. "I'd better get on my way. Lots to do on Goosefeather Farm this time of year."

"Thanks again, Abel." As his friend drove away, Jacob kicked at a clump of overgrown grass. Well, it looked like things at the church were finally coming to a head, and at the worst possible time. He had other things to worry about just now.

His upcoming talk with Natalie wasn't going to be pleasant.

The news he'd brought would hurt her, and he hated that. It just didn't seem right for a sweet woman like Natalie to be hurt, over and over again.

Of course, it also wasn't right that he'd hung up the phone with Bailey's park ranger friend this afternoon with a sharp flame of hope burning in his belly. It wasn't right that when he should be focused on what was best for Natalie, Ethan and Adam, Jacob's mind kept drifting selfishly toward what this news might mean for *him*.

"Jacob?"

He looked behind him. Natalie was picking her way across the rough yard, Ethan in her arms. His heart gave a thud that hurt all the way down to his feet.

She had her hair in some sort of sideways ponytail today, tumbling over her left shoulder, and she was dappled with the flickering shadows of the budding leaves above her. The sunlight sneaked through to tease gold glints out of her hair and highlight the soft fuzz just visible on Ethan's little head. She stepped carefully, her slender fingers protectively pressing her baby to her body.

She was wearing another one of the outfits he'd bought for her, and he felt a sudden, fierce possessiveness rise up in him. He wanted to do more of that. He wanted to buy her pretty things that made her smile and fill her cupboards with healthy food. He wanted to take care of Natalie and Ethan, pushing himself between them and anything that tried to hurt them.

Halfway between the goat pen and the house, Natalie stumbled over a rock, and Jacob was startled out of his thoughts. "Careful there."

He headed in her direction, and she stopped where she was, her fingers gently kneading Ethan's blanket. Her eyes focused intently on his face as he approached.

"Did you find Adam?"

"Natalie, let's go back inside and sit down. Okay?"

"No." She shook her head stubbornly. "Just go ahead and tell me now. Please. Whatever it is." She took a deep breath. "I can handle it."

There was a firmness in her voice that told him she meant to stand her ground. "Then let me hold Ethan, Natalie."

Worry leapt into her eyes, but after only a second's hesitation, she allowed him to take the baby from her arms. He settled Ethan against his chest, tucking in the blanket carefully.

He was stalling, and they both knew it.

"Tell me."

"A park ranger found Adam on the trail. Finally. It took some doing." Jacob paused, very aware of the soft, warm weight of the baby in his arms. There was no kind way to say this, so he might as well stop looking for one. "Adam saw all your messages about the baby, Natalie. He's just…not coming back."

She stared at him for a second, her expression blank. Then without a word, she turned and headed for the house.

He followed, cushioning Ethan against him. The baby was wide-awake, but he wasn't fussing. His unfocused eyes were wide with wonder, and Jacob could tell that soon they would be the same warm shade of brown as Natalie's. The little guy was growing so fast. He already looked different than he had those first minutes after his birth, those special minutes that Jacob had only experienced because Ethan's real father was out somewhere on a hiking trail eating beef jerky and communing with a pine tree.

Adam Larkey, Jacob thought for the umpteenth time, had some seriously messed-up priorities.

Natalie didn't say a word until they were back in the well-scrubbed kitchen. As Ethan stretched his feet in his bouncy chair, she turned to Jacob and cleared her throat.

"Thank you for finding Adam for me."

"I'm sorry it wasn't better news." And he *was* sorry—sorry that Natalie was hurt. But his regret didn't stretch much further than that. "Are you all right?"

"Yes." She nodded too forcefully, and her voice sounded strained. "After all, it's not like this is a big surprise." She turned away from him and started rearranging the items on the counter.

"Are you still in love with him, Natalie?"

He hadn't meant to ask her that. But somehow the question had just *come*, and now he needed the answer as badly as he needed air.

He saw her go suddenly still, saw her slender shoulders stiffen. She was staring down at a dish towel she clutched in her hand. It was faded, and it had a hole in it.

She needed new towels, but that wasn't all Natalie Davis needed. She needed new dreams, new plans, a whole new *life*. Surely, she'd be able to see that now.

He went to stand beside her. "Are you, Natalie?" His own voice sounded strange in his ears, rough with feelings he couldn't even put names to. "Because I think you deserve a lot more than Adam seems willing to give you."

She looked at him, her face tight. "It doesn't matter what I deserve."

"Of course it matters."

She shook her head fiercely. "You don't understand. It doesn't matter how I feel or what I want, not anymore. This whole mess is all my fault."

"No, it isn't."

"Yes, it *is*. I was so lonely. And I was working so hard and making no money, and I didn't have anybody to care about. Then Adam came into the restaurant, and he made me laugh. And I just…didn't want to be lonely anymore." She broke off, shaking her head again. "I knew Adam never wanted to get married. He's not that kind of guy. The minute I told him about the baby, he left."

"I'm not surprised." Running away seemed to be Larkey's response to just about everything.

"I called his grandmother about a month later. She was the only relative I knew how to find, and I didn't know what else to do. When I told her what had happened, she said some pretty… sharp things. But then she told me that she'd put money in a college fund for my baby *if* Adam and I were married. He needed to settle down, she said, and anyway, she didn't like the idea of her great-grandchild being raised in a housing project by a single mother. So she offered to give us this farm to live on. It all sounded so perfect."

"Natalie." He said her name and stopped. He had no idea what to say next.

It didn't really matter because Natalie rushed on. "I was scared and desperate, so I agreed if she could talk Adam into it. Do you know, it took nearly five months for her to convince him? And even then, she only managed it by threatening to cut off his allowance." Natalie laughed, but there was no humor in the sound. "I should have backed out then, I guess. But… I'd become a Christian by then, and marrying Adam seemed like the right thing to do. I mean, I really believed if I had faith and trusted God, He would work everything out."

"He always does, Natalie. Just sometimes not the way we want Him to."

"Like I told you, this isn't about what I want. Anyway, the main thing I want is for Ethan to have a good life. My own mom wasn't the most responsible person in the world." To Jacob's ears, that sounded like an understatement. "She couldn't hold down a job, so we never had enough money. It was so embarrassing. We were always having to ask people—" She broke off abruptly, her gaze flickering away from his. "Anyway, I don't want Ethan to go through that. I'm sorry. I really don't want to talk about all this right now, Jacob. Even though I was kind of expecting this, it's still hard. I have a lot of things to think about."

"I understand. And I can help, Natalie. I—"

"I don't want you doing me any more of your favors, Jacob. From what I hear, neither one of us can afford that right now."

"Natalie—" He reached out for her, but she brushed past him. She gathered Ethan swiftly out of his seat and fled into the nursery.

He stood where he was for a while, looking at the closed door. Then he leaned over and picked the ragged towel off the floor. He folded it carefully and placed it on the table. When he came back, he would bring her some new towels. Prettier ones.

Because he *was* coming back.

Natalie had told him a lot just now, but there was one very important thing she hadn't told him.

She hadn't told him she was still in love with Adam Larkey.

Natalie sat with Ethan cuddled against her shoulder, forcing herself to rock at a gentle pace as tears streamed down her cheeks. She heard Jacob shut the front door, heard his truck sputter to a start and crunch out onto the road.

For once, she was glad he'd gone. Jacob unsettled her. He made it hard to think clearly, and she needed to pull herself together.

Crying over this was silly. She'd suspected for some time now that Adam had no intention of keeping his promise. Wasn't that why she'd cut the blueberry deal with Bailey and taken the job at the coffee shop? Because she'd figured this was where she'd end up, fending for herself. Again. She should have been prepared for this news; she should have accepted it calmly.

No wonder Jacob had asked her if she was still in love with Adam. But this wasn't really about Adam.

And she wasn't in love with him. Jacob's pointed question had made her realize that, clear as day. What she'd felt for Adam, even way back at the beginning, hadn't really been love. Loneliness, yes, and desperation and a frantic grabbing at something to fill the emptiness inside her heart. But not love.

Love felt different. She knew that now.

She didn't want to think too hard about exactly *how* she knew it, but she did.

She raised her arm carefully so as not to disturb her baby and wiped her eyes on her sleeve. She couldn't sit here sniffling. She had Ethan to look after, and he needed her to be strong. He was depending on her to provide for him.

She'd have to find another full-time waitressing job. That would mean long, late hours, so she'd have to find a babysitter willing to keep Ethan well into the night on the days she had to close. She wouldn't be able to pay much, so her childcare options were going to be pretty grim. And where were they going to live? She'd have to leave Lark Hill. She hated the idea of moving back in to a housing project, but what other choice did she have?

She pressed her cheek against the fuzzy curve of her baby's head and closed her eyes. *Lord, Jacob's right. You sure don't always answer our prayers the way we want You to. I've tried so hard to make my plans work out, but everything just keeps getting worse. It looks like Your plan is a whole lot different from what I was expecting. Whatever it is, I hope You'll help me figure it out, because I sure seem to be making a lot of wrong turns lately. Please. For Ethan's sake. Work all this out for our good somehow. Amen.*

She stayed where she was for a few minutes, rocking. Little by little, her heartbeat slowed into its regular rhythm. Now that she'd officially given this over to God, she actually felt a little bit relieved.

She was still scared, but what she'd told Jacob was true. How she felt didn't really matter. She had to focus on putting one foot in front of the other until God revealed His plan, whatever that might be.

In the meantime, she might as well get busy and pick some blueberries.

Two days later, as she and Ethan drove away from Bailey's store, her car started acting up again. Natalie's heart skipped a beat, but then she cranked up the radio to drown out the rattling noise and kept right on counting her blessings.

Her first blueberry delivery couldn't have gone better. Bailey had been delighted with the berries. She'd sampled several immediately before weighing them and counting cash out of her register.

The money Bailey had given her wasn't much, but it was a start. And now that she was making plans to move back to Atlanta, she was going to need every penny of it.

As she drove through downtown Pine Valley, Natalie's eyes scanned the scene around her. Spring was in full force now. All along the sidewalks, flowers spilled over their planters in colorful riots. Encouraged by the beautiful weather, people lingered to chat in front of the various stores.

She loved this charming little town, and she hated the thought of leaving it. But it looked like that was exactly what she was going to have to do.

Yesterday, she'd broken down and called her old manager to see if he had any shift openings at the diner. He'd told her the new waitress he'd hired wasn't working out. Natalie could have her old job back, if she wanted it.

She didn't. But unfortunately, she needed it.

She really didn't want to move back into the housing project either, but rent in Atlanta was steep. She did know of one apartment complex that rented studios. She and Ethan would be cramped, but it was in a slightly better area. If she could sell enough blueberries, maybe, just maybe, she could swing the deposit and the first month's rent.

She glanced at the church steeple soaring up between the old oaks, then looked quickly away. As long as she and Ethan had each other, they'd be fine.

They didn't need anybody else.

A horn sounded behind her. Startled, she glanced into her rearview mirror to see Jacob waving at her from the cab of his truck. He flashed his lights and motioned toward the church parking lot. He wanted her to pull over.

Her heart sank when she caught a glimpse of the determined look on his face. She'd been avoiding him ever since he'd told her the news about Adam. If she didn't pull into that parking lot, Jacob was perfectly capable of following her all the way out to Lark Hill with his hazards flashing.

She could just imagine what the members of his congregation would make of *that*.

Natalie pulled over but left her engine running. She watched in her side mirror as Jacob pulled in behind her, rolling down the window as he approached.

His eyes looked sea blue in the light of the spring day, and his golden hair shone. Her stomach dipped, and she clenched the steering wheel a little tighter. "Your engine's skipping."

"It's still running, though. That's the important thing." She didn't want him trying to arrange more repairs, so she changed the subject quickly. "I just made my first blueberry delivery to Bailey's."

"That's great!" Pause. "How's…uh… Rufus?"

Funny. Jacob seemed a little nervous.

"Same as always. Out of his pen every time I turn around." She hesitated, but there was really no way around what she needed to say next. "Do you think you could find me a home for him? You offered before, remember?"

"Sure, and the offer stands. It may take me a few days, though. Rufus is pretty notorious around here."

"I hope you can find him a good place. He can be a nuisance, but I'm really going to miss him when I go back to Atlanta. That'll be in a couple of weeks, give or take, as soon as I get all these blueberries picked off. So you'd better start thinking about who around here owes you the biggest favor." She forced another smile, but this time Jacob didn't smile back.

"You and I need to talk, Natalie."

"I'm kind of in a hurry, Jacob. Ethan's over-due for his nap, and…"

"Please."

Natalie sighed. "Okay." She turned the key in the ignition, silencing her engine. Hopefully, it would start up again when she needed it to. Smack-dab in front of Jacob's church was the last place she needed to get stranded. "What do you want to talk about?"

Instead of answering, he rounded the car and opened the back door. Before she could protest, he began unfastening the carrier part of Ethan's car seat from its base.

"Jacob," she protested. "I really only have a minute. Can't we talk here?"

"No." He headed toward the church with the baby carrier swinging gently from one arm, leaving her no alternative but to trot behind him.

To her surprise, once inside the church, he didn't turn left down the hall that led to his office. He went straight through the big doors into the empty sanctuary. He walked down the center aisle, carrying Ethan toward the front of the church.

She'd never been inside a church when it was completely empty before. The vaulted room was hushed, and their steps were muffled by the thick carpet. The sun flowed silently through the stained glass windows, spattering quivering cubes of colored light all over the white walls.

Pine Valley Community Church wasn't fancy. The windows were only colored squares, not Bible pictures, and the pews were plain blond oak. But it had a peaceful, welcoming air that she liked.

Strange how friendly churches could feel when they were empty.

Jacob led her to the front pew, where she'd sat during the service, and set Ethan's carrier carefully on the floor.

He sat, and she sank slowly down beside him. His eyes found hers, and there was such a strange, dogged look in them that she forgot all about herself and her problems.

She leaned forward and rested her hands lightly over his. "Jacob, what is it?"

His fingers tightened around hers with a strength that surprised her. "I'd like to talk to you about staying in Pine Valley."

Chapter Twelve

He had his reasons all ready. In fact, he'd probably spent more time preparing for this conversation than he had for his first sermon.

Natalie didn't give him a chance.

She pulled her hands free of his and stood up. "There's nothing to talk about, Jacob. Trust me, I've looked at this from every angle. There's just no way it works. Now, I'm sorry, but I really do have to get back." She reached for the handle of Ethan's baby carrier.

"Natalie, please." He stood up, too. "Wait." He had a feeling if he let her walk out that door now, she'd be walking right out of his life. "At least hear me out. I think you owe me that much."

He knew the minute the words were out of his mouth. It was exactly the wrong thing to say.

She turned back toward him. "I owe you?"

"That's not what I meant, Natalie. It's a figure of speech."

"But in this case, it's true, isn't it? I really do owe you. In fact—" She pulled a folded wad of bills out of her pocket, peeled off some and held them out. "Here. I know this is just a drop in the bucket, but consider it a down payment. I'll get you the rest when I can."

He made no move to accept the money. This discussion sure had gone south in a hurry. "Natalie, please. That came out all wrong. Can we start over?"

"You know what? I wish we could." Her voice thrummed with so much feeling that he knew she wasn't just talking about this conversation. "This time I'd know better than to rack up debts I have no way of repaying." She set the cash down on the pew.

"I don't want your money, Natalie. I never did. Be fair. You're the one who kept insisting on repaying me. I know you *feel* like you owe me, but you don't. That's not the way this works. We're—" he fumbled for the right word, and had to settle on one that didn't quite cover it "—friends. Friends don't have to pay each other back."

"I may not be as educated as you are, Jacob, but I'm pretty sure you're wrong about that.

Friends do pay each other back. They help each other. And that's how I know we're not friends."

He stared at her. "What are you talking about?"

"You! Me!" She made a frustrated gesture. "This! What you've been giving me isn't friendship, Jacob. It's charity. I know you're using my situation to make a point with your church board, but—"

"*What?* Who told you that?" If it was Arlene, so help him…

"That's not important. What's important is that *you* didn't tell me. You didn't tell me about all the trouble you've been having with this Digby guy or about how you could maybe even lose your job. In all the time we've spent together, you never even brought it up. You've been helping me with my problems ever since we met, but I didn't even *know* about yours. That seems pretty one-sided to me, Jacob."

He shook his head. "You're wrong."

"Am I?" She started ticking things off on her fingers. "You've spent money I know you couldn't spare buying me groceries and a whole baby nursery and clothes. You paid to have my car fixed. You drove me to the hospital and stayed with me when Ethan was born. You've fixed crazy Rufus's fence more times than I can count. You've changed diapers, and cleaned up spit-up, and you even located Adam for me. Not that it did much good."

"And you think you *owe* me for all that?" The sharpness in his tone finally caught her attention. She stopped, her lips parted, staring at him. "If anything, I owe you. I loved doing all those things." She slanted him a skeptical look. "I did. Why is that so hard to believe? You think you're the only person who knows what it's like to be lonely? You're not. Before you and Ethan came along there was a hole in my life you could drive a truck through."

"Lonely? *You?*" At least now she was listening to him. Her eyes searched his. "I find that a little hard to believe."

"It's true. You remember when we met you told me you didn't have much family? Well, I don't have much family, either. My parents died in a car accident not long after I got out of college. The closest relatives I have are a set of second cousins who live in Oregon. I haven't seen them in years."

"You never told me that."

"You never asked."

He watched the play of emotions across her face. "I'm sorry. You're right. I didn't."

"It's okay. I understood. You had plenty of your own stuff to worry about. But the truth is, Natalie, I haven't had anything resembling a real family for years. I've filled up that space in my life with my work, with my church family. I've stayed late with them at hospitals and funeral parlors. I've driven them to their cancer treatments. I've helped them move, and I've babysat their hyperactive Labradoodles so they could take their kids to Disney World. I've spent my weekends painting Sunday school classrooms and fishing broken crayons out of the church nursery sink. And that's all fine and good, but you know what the problem with that is?"

Natalie shook her head.

"Sooner or later you have to go home. You have to go back to an empty apartment, to eat some stupid microwave meal by yourself, and then stare at the walls until it's time to go back to work again. And trust me, that's not nearly as much fun as I'm making it sound."

A smile flickered across her face, but she nodded seriously. "You don't have to tell me. I know what it's like, being alone."

"Then you should understand why I've loved every single minute I've spent with you and Ethan. It felt almost like…having a family of my own." He offered her a small, careful smile. "Spit-up, dirty diapers, crazy fence-busting goat and all."

It worked. She smiled wider. "All that's not as much fun as you make it sound, either."

She was joking back with him. This was progress. "It is to me. And I'm sorry I didn't tell you about the stuff going on here at the church. But it wasn't because I wanted our relationship to be one-sided, and it definitely wasn't because I was using you to make some kind of ethical point to my board. I didn't even want to think about this church when I was with you. You and Lark Hill and Ethan were my escape." He stopped and looked around the quiet sanctuary. "Don't get me wrong. I love this place, and I love every single member of my congregation. But I'll admit, there are some of them I don't *like* all that much." Natalie laughed softly, and he smiled.

He loved to hear her laugh.

"I'm sorry," he added, even though he wasn't. "I guess that's a rotten thing for a minister to say."

She shook her head. "No, don't apologize. I understand."

"Trust me. I don't want to talk to you about staying in town because I'm so charitable. If anything, I want to help you stay because I'm so selfish. Because I can't stand the thought of my life going back to the way it was before you and Ethan came here." He waited a few seconds, trying unsuccessfully to read her expression.

"Well, we have that in common, I guess,"

Natalie admitted finally. "I'm not too excited about going back to the way my life used to be, either."

"Then stay." She still looked unsure. "Will you at least pray about it?"

She hesitated, then nodded. "Okay. Yes. I'll pray about it. If this works out…well, it might be a good thing for Ethan. Once there was this neighbor who had a little girl about my age. My mom…wasn't home much, so I used to stay at their apartment a lot. I called him Uncle Steve, and he kind of looked out for me. He helped me with my homework and let me eat supper at their house sometimes. I really missed that when he got a better job, and they moved away. I'd like Ethan to have somebody like that in his life, somebody like you, I mean. I think it'd be…nice."

It didn't sound nice to Jacob. It sounded sad. But she was leaning toward staying, and he should just leave well enough alone.

But still. An honorary uncle.

That had three-legged turtle written all over it.

"Natalie? I'd love to be a part of Ethan's life. That'd be great. But…that's not all I'm asking you to consider here. I want to be a part of *your* life, too."

She'd leaned over, reaching for the baby

carrier again, but she froze. She straightened and turned back in his direction. The silence stretched on long enough that it made him a little uneasy.

Natalie nibbled on her lower lip, the way she tended to do when she was uncertain. Finally, she said, a little too lightly, "Well, sure. If I stay, we'll be friends, too, you and I. Real friends, this time, though. No more one-sided stuff." She paused. "That's…what you're talking about. Isn't it?"

"Yes." He hesitated, but he had to be honest. "Absolutely. To start with. But I was hoping, maybe…" Good grief, this was hard to put into words. "That in time…when you're ready…that our friendship could lead to…possibly…something else."

That shock on her face wasn't exactly encouraging. Wait, surely she didn't think he meant…

"Of course, my intentions are…you know, completely honorable." He winced. "Sorry, that sounded really stupid."

And people wondered why he was still single.

"No. Not stupid." Natalie still looked a little taken aback, but at least the color was coming back into her cheeks. "A little…crazy, maybe. But not stupid." She hesitated, her eyes still locked with his. She didn't seem to know exactly what to say. "I'll…uh…"

"Pray about it," he finished hopefully.

"Yes." She nodded, still looking a little dazed. "Right. I will."

"Good." He looked down at Ethan, snuggled in the car seat, sound asleep. He was sporting a bib Jacob had picked out, one with a red airplane zooming across its terry cloth front. "I'll carry Ethan out to the car for you."

"No." Natalie blinked. "No, I've got him. Thanks, though." She picked up the carrier and started for the door.

Halfway up the aisle, she halted, looking back at him. "And just so you know, Jacob, I think you're the least selfish person I've ever met."

Jacob stayed where he was and watched until the oversize door thumped shut behind her. Then he sank back down on the pew. He might as well stay right here.

Natalie wasn't the only one who had some praying to do.

The following Thursday afternoon, Jacob sneaked a glance at his watch under the meeting room table. Quarter till six, and so far the church board spent the whole time dithering over what type of hardwood floors should be installed in the fellowship hall, and whether the finish should be English Oak or Walnut Bronze.

Jacob had blanched when he'd caught sight of

the estimate for the flooring. Just as he'd feared, this building project was getting more ambitious—and costly—by the day. He'd tried twice to interject some common sense into the discussion, but Abel Whitlock had been the only member to back him up. The rest of them seemed solidly in Digby's camp.

In any case, he knew the whole floor debate was nothing but a smoke screen. The church board members kept shooting uneasy glances in Jacob's direction, but nobody had been brave enough to bring up the real reason for this meeting yet.

Fortunately, he wasn't the only one getting restless. "All right, now. I reckon we've talked nonsense long enough." Abel Whitlock shifted in his chair. "We might as well get along to the point of this meeting, so we can all go home."

"Maybe we should postpone." High school principal Andrew Carlton darted another nervous look in Jacob's direction. "It's getting late."

"Oh no, you don't. I'm not about to waste another perfectly good spring afternoon cooped up inside because none of you have the guts to speak plain. Like I told you before, I don't hold with talking behind people's backs. Somebody say whatever it is you came here to say, and let's get this over with. I've got my milk cow to see to."

A strained silence fell across the table as the twelve members of the board looked at each other.

"Fine. If nobody else will say it, I will." Digby Markham spoke up from his strategic position at the end of the long table. "The truth is, Jacob, we met this afternoon to discuss your lack of support for this fellowship hall project. We made it clear to you that this would be the primary focus of the church for the foreseeable future and that you'd need to make it your top priority. You don't appear to have listened."

Digby Markham was accusing *him* of not listening? That was ironic. Jacob took a deep breath and tried to hang on to the shreds of his patience. "I'm sorry you feel that way, Digby. And if the church is determined to build this thing, I'll certainly be as supportive as I can be. But the truth is, I don't believe that the primary focus of any church should be building itself a fancy fellowship hall."

"But it's an investment," young Darren Ellerbee spoke up earnestly. "If we build a really nice one, we can rent it out for weddings and other events and recoup our money."

"We're a church, not a convention center," Jacob pointed out. "I think—"

"That debate is closed," Digby interrupted. "We've already heard enough about what you think, Stone. The decision's been made, and you need to get in line."

"Come on, Digby." Jack Lifsey, who ran the local feed store, darted a worried look at Jacob as he spoke. "Settle down. We're all on the same team, here, aren't we?"

"That's my question. Are we?" Digby raised an eyebrow and looked at Jacob. "From what I hear, you're playing for Good Shepherd's team these days."

"What?" Jacob had been prepared for Digby to say just about anything at this meeting, but that was a surprise.

"It's the only way your recent behavior adds up. The Larkeys have always attended Good Shepherd. Everybody knows that. From what I've heard, Cora Larkey is one of their biggest financial supporters, and I know for a fact she has no intention of moving any of that support to Pine Valley Community. And Pastor Michaelson's getting mighty close to his retirement, and he's had a terrible time getting over that flu he had." Digby sat back in his chair and steepled his fingers in front of his stomach with an air of satisfaction. "*That's* why you skipped out on your responsibilities here to help him out at that Larkey wedding. And of course, that's the reason you don't support our church building a nice fellowship hall. You're planning to jump ship."

A hubbub of alarmed voices broke out around the conference table.

"Is that true?"

"Are you leaving us to preach for Good Shepherd?"

"Of course not," Jacob assured the agitated men.

"Oh no?" Digby leveled a challenging glare across the table. "Why else would you be spending so much time out at Lark Hill hovering over that woman Adam Larkey dumped at the altar? It's the only explanation I can think of that makes sense."

"It's not the only one I can think of." Abel Whitlock sounded amused, and Jacob shot him an exasperated look.

Too late. Digby raised his eyebrows. "I hope you're not suggesting that the pastor of our church has a romantic interest in an unmarried mother. Especially not one who's supposedly planning to marry another man. That's just about the only thing I can think of worse than the explanation I've already come up with."

Heads swiveled in Jacob's direction, waiting for his denial. All except for Abel, who'd turned brick red and looked like he wished he'd stayed home and milked his cow.

Jacob tried to think of a way to balance discretion and truth in his response. "Natalie's engagement to Adam Larkey didn't work out," he said finally.

He hadn't denied it. The men shifted uncomfortably in their chairs and looked at each other. Nobody seemed to know what to say.

"This," Digby pronounced solemnly, "is precisely why no minister should be unmarried. My nephew, for instance, made it a point to find a suitable young woman before he graduated from seminary. *His* future congregation will never have to deal with a scandal like this."

"Don't exaggerate, Digby." Andrew Carlton spoke with the authority of a man who managed teenagers for a living. "It's not like Jacob had a child out of wedlock himself." He chuckled drily. "Now *that* would be a scandal."

The room went suddenly very still. Half the men in the room, the ones who knew about Jacob's past, exchanged significant glances. Digby straightened up in his chair, suddenly alert, and Carlton looked from one man to another, his brow furrowed.

"What? Is there something I don't know about?"

Oh brother. Might as well get this over with. "Apparently there is, Andrew. Before I became a Christian, my college girlfriend and I gave a baby up for adoption."

"Which doesn't matter worth a hill of beans to us right now," Abel spoke up from his corner.

"Well, of course, *you'd* say that, Whitlock, since your own wife—"

"I'd stop right there if I were you, Markham." Abel's voice was quiet, almost lazy, but there was an unmistakable thread of steel in it.

Digby started to speak, then took another look at Abel and thought better of it. He turned back to Jacob. "Well, this explains the attachment you seem to have to Natalie Davis. Birds of a feather, I suppose."

"But we're all birds, Digby," Carlton put in, casting an apologetic look toward Jacob. "None of us are perfect, and we've certainly all made our share of mistakes."

"And some of us seem determined to keep right on making them, apparently." When the principal tried to interrupt him, Digby waved an impatient hand. "No, Andrew, it's time for us to speak bluntly. I didn't hear Stone denying that he's got a personal interest in this Davis woman."

"Now, now. The preacher has a right to his personal life, Digby," Jack Lifsey put in. "And anyhow, you were just saying yourself that you didn't hold with bachelor ministers."

"Yes, but in this case, the woman is completely unsuitable. No, Andrew, don't shush me. You finally want to find yourself a girl and get married, Stone? Fine. We're all for it. There are plenty of decent women in Pine Valley for you to choose from. A fact you ought to know since our wives have pretty much introduced you to every single one of them over the past few years. You've never shown the slightest interest, and now you're chasing after a woman like Natalie Davis? Of course, now that I know your own history, I'm a lot less surprised."

"You know, you're stomping around on some mighty thin ice, Digby." Abel studied his fingernails. "Take it from me, a man's words can get him into a peck of trouble, if he's not careful. Even a preacher has his limits."

Jacob realized his fists were clenched in his lap, and he forced himself to relax them. *Lord, help me keep my cool.*

"Stone's the one who'd better be careful. This board has its limits, too."

"Digby—" Several voices protested at once. The banker shook his head stubbornly.

"This man has given us more than enough trouble already. We wouldn't be looking at so much fund-raising now if he hadn't spent the last few years throwing away all our money on coffee shops and prison outreaches and mission trips to all sorts of nasty places. And now he's taking up with a woman like that? It's shameful, is what it is. I say let Good Shepherd have him. If we don't draw a line now, where's it going to end?"

"I can answer that question." Jacob stood. He'd had enough. More than enough. "It's going to end right here. Right now. You'll find my resignation in your in-boxes tomorrow morning." He left the room before any of them recovered enough to speak.

In fact, he was almost out of the church before Abel Whitlock caught up with him. "Whoa, there." He turned to face the lanky farmer, who scanned his face quickly. Abel nodded slowly. "All right then. It wasn't just temper. No point in my asking you if you meant what you said back there. I can see plain enough that you did."

"Every word."

"If I'd kept my trap shut, it might not have come to this. I'm sorry, Jacob. You know me— I'm always sticking my foot in my mouth."

Abel looked sincerely troubled, and Jacob clapped his friend on the back. "Don't worry about it. It was going to have to be dealt with sooner or later. Might as well get it over with."

"So she's something special to you, is she? This Natalie?"

"She is." Jacob nodded, and in spite of everything, he could feel the grin spreading across his face. "She really is."

"Well, that'll make it a mite easier to see you go, I reckon. For some of us, anyway. But all the same, I'd count it as a personal favor if you wouldn't let on that I had anything to do with it. Folks around here are right fond of you, Digby Markham notwithstanding. Including my Emily." Abel tilted his head toward the conference room, where a rumble of raised voices could be heard. "And she's not the only one. I imagine Digby's catching it right about now."

Jacob chuckled. Now that his decision had finally been made, his heart was feeling lighter than it had in a long time. "To be honest, I hope he is." He offered Abel his hand. "Thanks for giving me the heads-up about this meeting, Whitlock. I appreciate it."

Abel accepted the handshake with a firm grip and a nod. As Jacob followed his friend through the door, he automatically paused to give it the extra tug it always required to shut all the way.

He stood there for a minute, his hand resting on the familiar dented handle. Then he took a deep breath, turned away from the church and headed for his truck.

The blueberries were ripening too fast.

Natalie stripped the heavy twig of its dusky

blueberries and moved quickly on. She'd only visited half a dozen bushes, and her pail was already brimming. Even worse, the ground was studded with overripe fruit. She wasn't keeping up.

There had to be a more efficient way to do this, but she had no idea what it might be. Plucking each berry off its stem individually was taking forever. No wonder blueberries were so stinking expensive in the grocery store. She sure hoped Bailey was charging a mint for these.

She edged around the large bush picking as quickly as she could, Ethan contentedly snuggled in the baby sling she'd wrapped around her middle. Ever since she'd cut her deal with Bailey Quinn, Natalie had been praying that God would bless these bushes.

Well, he'd definitely answered.

She stopped and looked around. Bushes stretched in every direction, and every branch sagged with berries. As best she could tell, most of the unripe ones would turn blue at roughly the same time.

Soon.

She had no idea what she was going to do about that, not with a baby to look after and her part-time job to go to. Even if she picked twenty-four hours a day, she didn't think she could get even half the berries off the bushes before they spoiled.

And Bailey was counting on these berries. She'd sent some samples to restaurants, and she'd shown Natalie the stack of orders that had come back. She couldn't disappoint Bailey. Not to mention that Natalie needed every penny of the money Bailey would pay her.

She couldn't stay at Lark Hill much longer, not now that she knew Adam wasn't coming back. If she returned to Atlanta, she'd need the money for the deposit on that studio apartment. Then again… She wondered what the going rent was in Pine Valley. If she stayed…

If she stayed. Every time those words came into her mind, which was frequently, her heart gave a weird little lurch.

Her heart had been doing all kinds of strange things ever since the conversation she'd had with Jacob. She'd been trying to think it over, to pray, like she'd promised, but she hadn't gotten very far.

She still couldn't quite wrap her mind around what Jacob had said. The idea that a man like him, a minister no less, was even a little bit interested in a woman who got a case of the shudders every time she went inside a church… Well. It was kind of hard to believe.

But she wanted to believe it. She really did.

The problem was, she just didn't see how it could work out, not unless something changed.

The goat suddenly bleated, and she jumped. She had absentmindedly left the blueberry field and wandered back up toward the farmhouse. Typical. Every time her mind revisited those moments in the church sanctuary, her feelings rose up in one big fluttering cloud, and her brain went on vacation.

Rufus had escaped again, and he wanted to see what she had in her pail. She offered him a couple of blueberries. He gobbled them up greedily, leaving a smear of purple juice on her fingers.

"What do you think? Should I stay, Rufus?" The goat blatted at her again, straining to get to the bucket she'd lifted out of range. He chewed on a fold of Ethan's sling instead. Natalie took a step backward, and the goat snorted at her irritably.

"Natalie?"

She glanced in the direction of the house, and her heart went still.

Adam was standing in the side yard, his battered green knapsack on the ground beside his feet. An unfamiliar car was parked sideways in front of the house.

"Adam?" She stood there frozen. Beside her, Rufus tensed. His neck stretched in Adam's direction, and his floppy ears twitched. Suddenly, the goat took off at a gallop, heading for Adam at full speed. "Rufus!"

"Hey, buddy! Looks like somebody is glad to see me." Adam held one hand out. "No hard feelings about me taking off, right?"

Rufus never slowed down. He lowered his head and butted Adam squarely in the stomach, knocking him flat onto the ground.

"Adam! Are you all right? Rufus! Bad goat!" Pressing Ethan against her, Natalie set down her pail and hurried as quickly as she could to where Adam lay prone in the grass, coughing and gasping for air. Rufus pranced around him, pawing the earth and snorting.

"Wow." Adam levered himself up on one elbow and watched Rufus uneasily. "That dude holds a serious grudge."

Natalie stood over him, looking down at the man she'd almost married. His light brown hair was tousled and long. He was wearing some sort of twine bracelet tied around his wrist and a mud-colored T-shirt that said Live Life Lazy. He stared up at her, his hazel eyes round with surprise. His lips were chapped, and the end of his nose was a delicate pink.

He looked about twelve years old.

His face is too soft, Natalie thought. Jacob's was different. Not hard exactly, but firmer and stronger somehow, even with those dimples of his.

Adam clambered to his feet and brushed off his cargo shorts. Ethan shifted and whimpered against her, and Adam took an involuntary step back. Then he glanced at Natalie with an embarrassed expression.

"That the little guy?"

"Yes, this is Ethan." Natalie felt a strange reluctance, but she carefully folded back the fabric of the sling so that Adam could see the baby's face. Ethan blinked his eyes and worked his mouth before falling back to sleep. With the sunlight on his round cheek, and his wisps of baby-fine hair standing out like a halo, he looked adorable. Natalie's heart swelled with love and pride.

Adam craned over to peek at the infant, but he didn't move closer. "Wow. He's really tiny." Rufus gave a warning snort, and Adam took another uneasy step backward. "Hey, Nat, you got anything to eat in the house? I'm starving."

Tiny. That was Adam's only reaction to his son? Natalie's mind slipped back to Jacob rocking Ethan in the hospital, his tired face full of wonder as he looked at the sleeping newborn.

She blinked and came back to the present. "Sure, there's food. Come on inside. Not you," she added as Rufus made a move to follow them. The goat gave her one last, disgusted look, then trotted off to gobble up the berries in her abandoned pail.

In the kitchen, she settled Ethan in his bouncy seat while Adam rummaged through the refrigerator. He tossed containers of food on the table, jerking open drawers until he found a fork. He wiped his nose on his shirtsleeve and dropped his lanky frame into a chair.

He cracked open the plastic tub of chicken salad and began eating directly out of the full container. Natalie felt a flash of annoyance. Adam did things like that. Drank out of the milk cartons, left his trash lying around. He didn't just look like a kid; he acted like one, too.

A confusion of emotions jostled around in Natalie's stomach as she pulled out a chair and sat across the table from him. She didn't know what to think, and she definitely didn't have a clue how to feel right now.

"This stuff is really good. I've been sick, so I've been off my chow for a while. I'm just now starting to get my appetite back." That explained the runny nose and the stuffy sound to his voice. Natalie made a mental note to put any leftover chicken salad into the trash. "I've gotta say, the kitchen sure looks better than the way I left it. Sorry about that, by the way."

"I thought you weren't coming back." The words came out before she could stop them.

Adam paused in midchew. He glanced at her, then refocused on digging around in the container with his fork. "I wasn't."

"What changed your mind?"

Adam dropped his fork into the salad and pushed the plastic tub away. "Nana Cora. After that park ranger found me on the trail, I figured I might as well come back and check on Nana. You know, see how she was doing." He darted another quick glance up at Natalie's face as he spoke, probably to see if she was buying his explanation. She wasn't. She figured Adam's visit to Cora had a lot more to do with Adam's finances than his grandmother's health. "She's been sick, and she wasn't much in the mood for company, but before I left she made me promise to come out here and see you and, you know…" Adam nodded in Ethan's direction. "*Him*. Make sure you have everything you need." Adam's expression brightened a little. "Which, from the look of things, you do."

No thanks to you, Natalie added silently. "How is Cora doing? Last time I spoke to her, she was getting over the flu."

"Better. She's kind of in a wad, though, over you getting the church involved in family problems. She says she told you that wasn't a good idea, but you went ahead and did it anyhow."

Natalie felt a pang of guilt, but then straightened her shoulders and pushed it aside. This wasn't her fault. "If you'd come back when you'd said you would, or answered any of my texts, I wouldn't have had to ask the minister to find you, Adam."

"Yeah, well." Adam shifted uncomfortably in his chair. "That wasn't the part she was so upset about. She was mad because some guy called and got on her case about the preacher having to pay for your food and the baby's stuff."

Natalie stood up so fast that the legs of her chair screeched against the linoleum. Ethan startled in his bouncy seat and set up a thin wail of protest. "What?"

"Wow, Nat. Calm down, okay? She's already sent the dude a check, so it's all taken care of. But she made it pretty clear that's the last check she's planning to write. For either one of us."

Natalie gathered up her crying son then and sank back into her chair. She pressed Ethan against her, soothing him, and refocused her attention on Adam. Oddly, he didn't really seem that concerned. In fact, he looked more relaxed than she'd seen him since she told him about the baby. "How are you going to manage?"

"I'm getting by."

"How?"

"Uh." Adam glanced down at the table. "Well. You know."

"Oh." Natalie nodded slowly, remembering the unfamiliar car out front. Three guesses who that belonged to. "You met a woman."

"Yeah." He looked back up at her sheepishly. "I'm sorry, Nat. It's just…this whole family thing, it's just not me, you know? It never was. Darla doesn't ever want to get married or have any kids either, and she's got a little money from an uncle who died. The two of us just want to kick back and have a good time." He shot her another guilty look. "I feel bad about all this, Nat, I really do. I did care about you, and I never wanted to hurt you. But I just can't change who I am. I guess you think I'm kind of a jerk."

Natalie started to agree, then stopped herself. He made a good point.

Adam had never once pretended to be anything other than what he was, an irresponsible guy looking for an easy life and somebody to have fun with. She was the one who'd let her hopes and her loneliness run away with her, and look where it had gotten them.

"You know what? It's all right." Natalie reached across the table and touched Adam lightly on his arm. She nodded at him, holding his eyes with hers. "No hard feelings. Okay?"

"Okay." Adam brightened a little, considering her. "You've changed, Nat. You know that? And it's not just that you're totally rocking this baby thing. You're, like…different."

She was. She hadn't fully realized that until now.

There was a knock on the door. Natalie frowned. "Who could that be?" She stood and settled her drowsy son back into his little fabric seat. He'd probably be sound asleep in a few seconds. "Keep an eye on the baby. I'll be right back."

"Me?" Adam stared at his son with such an expression of horror that Natalie didn't know whether to laugh or sigh.

"I'll only be a minute."

She walked through the living room and opened the door. Jacob was standing on the porch.

A wave of awareness swept over her like a refreshing breeze. Seeing Jacob's face after the emotional roller coaster of Adam's return felt like slipping on comfortable shoes after a long day in pinchy heels. He was wearing his khakis and that rumpled blue shirt with the fraying collar. His hair had flopped over his forehead, and he was standing with most of his weight on his right leg, the way he always did.

She hadn't even realized that he did that until now.

He held a bouquet of daisies and pink roses in one hand, sheathed in green cellophane. The scent of the flowers mingled pleasantly with the spiciness of his soap.

She glanced down at the flowers and then up into his face. He smiled, and the tiny creases in the corners of his eyes deepened. He held the flowers out to her, and she accepted them automatically.

"You might as well know up front, those are a bribe. I know it's short notice, but I want you to have dinner with me. I've made reservations over in Fairmont and lined up a babysitter and everything." His dimples twinkled, and her stomach flipped over. "Not that I wouldn't enjoy spending some time with Ethan, but I'd kind of like your undivided attention tonight. There's something I really need to talk to you about. I guess I should have checked with you first, though. It looks like you've got company." He nodded in the direction of Adam's car. "Anybody I know?"

"It's a loaner, bro." Adam spoke from behind her, and she half turned to find him lounging against the doorway leading into the kitchen. "My old Jeep finally conked out."

Chapter Thirteen

"Adam." Jacob looked at Natalie's face. Her cheeks were flushed, and she wouldn't meet his gaze. He waited for a minute, but nobody spoke. "I'm sorry. Am I interrupting something?"

"Adam, could you go back into the kitchen with Ethan, please? Jacob and I need to talk." Natalie stepped out onto the porch and closed the door. "Jacob—"

"When did he get back?" The question came out before he could stop it.

"Just now."

"Is he staying?"

"Jacob…" Natalie repeated his name, then stopped. She had a pink shawl thrown over her narrow shoulders. He remembered it. It converted into an infant sling, and the lady at the Baby Superstore had assured him it was the latest thing in baby gear. He hadn't realized until

Natalie had laughed that he should probably have bought the blue one instead. He hadn't even thought about that; he'd just imagined how pretty Natalie would look in pink.

He'd been right. The rosy shade reflected color into her creamy cheeks and added warmth to her brown hair. She was wearing it down today, the way he liked best, and it curled loosely over her shoulders.

One of the ranging chickens squawked in the side yard, jerking Jacob back to the present. He repeated his question. "Is Adam staying?"

"If you mean here in the house with me, no." Natalie drew the shawl tighter around herself, even though the spring sun had the old porch so warm that the new lumber was releasing its sweet piney smell. "We're not married, and that wouldn't be right."

"I'm sorry, Natalie. I didn't mean—"

"That's okay," she said quickly, but her eyes told him a different story. His clumsy question had hurt her. "I can understand why you'd as-sume—"

"I didn't assume. I just wanted to know if Adam was planning to stay here in town."

"He hasn't told me much about his plans yet. Jacob, did you call Cora Larkey?"

He couldn't put his finger on it, but something about the way she asked the question made him feel like he was walking into a minefield. "Yes, I did. I called her when you asked me to look for Adam. I wanted to know if she knew anything that might help us pinpoint his exact location. The Appalachian Trail covers a lot of territory."

"Did you ask her for money?"

"What? No!" He stared at her, brow crinkled. "Of course not. Why?"

"Well, somebody from your church did. They wanted repayment for what you've spent on me."

It had to be Digby. Jacob suddenly recalled that remark the banker had tossed off in the meeting about Cora Larkey's plans to continue supporting Good Shepherd Church. *I know for a fact*, he'd said.

Digby knew for a fact because he'd talked to Cora himself. And he'd done more than talk to her, he'd tried to finagle some money out of her, probably so that he could add another expensive curlicue to that horrible fellowship hall he was so determined to build.

Under false pretenses, at that. None of the money Jacob had spent had come out of the church's funds. The irritation that Jacob always felt where Digby was concerned escalated into angry disgust, and he felt an overwhelming desire to punch something. Hard.

"I promise you, I had nothing to do with that,

Natalie." He took a deep breath. "And it's not my church anymore. I resigned."

"What?" Natalie's eyes widened. "Why? Because of the trouble with that fellowship hall?"

"That had a lot to do with it."

Her eyes searched his worriedly. "It didn't have anything to do with…what we talked about at the church, did it? Your decision to quit didn't involve me?"

Jacob felt a flash of frustration as he struggled with his answer. *Of course it involves you. Everything I do, almost every thought I have, involves you now.* He couldn't tell her that. Not with Adam waiting for her back in the house. But he couldn't lie to her, either.

So he stayed silent, and her face crumpled. "Oh."

"It's all right, Natalie."

"Nat?" Adam's voice called from inside the house. "Little dude's squawking, and I think he needs a cleanup. You'd better come here."

"I should probably go in." Natalie's voice didn't sound very steady. "Adam doesn't have a clue about babies."

Jacob didn't want to let her go, not now. Not leaving things like this between them. But he didn't see that he had much choice. "All right. But we need to talk."

The sound of a baby's fretful wail came from

the house, and Natalie looked over her shoulder. "I could come to your office, I guess. Tomorrow, maybe?"

"That's fine."

It was the first time he'd been less than honest with her. He realized that when he was halfway to his truck, when he heard her shut the door behind him.

Nothing was fine. Not until he knew for certain what Natalie was planning to do.

In his church office the following morning, Jacob was trying to start the process of packing. He figured that was as good a way as any to fill the time until Natalie came by.

Unfortunately, he was getting nowhere. Arlene stood beside him, her hands on her knobby hips, vibrating with worry. She watched as Jacob picked up a Popsicle stick picture frame and set it in one of the cardboard boxes he'd wheedled out of the supermarket manager.

Then she took it right back out and replaced it in its spot on the shelf. "This is ridiculous, Jacob."

"I've already sent in my resignation, Arlene. It's a done deal."

"Not if I have anything to say about it, it isn't. And I'm not the only one, either. Stop with the packing! We're going to get all this straightened out. A special meeting's already been called for Wednesday night."

Jacob winced. Not another special meeting. That was the last thing he needed right now. "I'm not sure that's such a good idea, Arlene."

"Well, anything's a better idea than this!" The waver in Arlene's voice made him glance sharply at her.

His take-no-prisoners secretary was crying.

Jacob cast a quick look out the window to see if the world had, in fact, come to an end without him realizing it. Then he took Arlene by the arm and led her to a chair. "Okay, now. Sit down, and let's talk about this."

"There's nothing to talk about. You're not leaving this church, and that's all there is to it." Arlene rummaged under the piles of paper on his desk until she found a half-squashed tissue box. She plucked one square out and blew her nose like a trumpet. "It's all the dust you're stirring up in here," she explained irritably, not looking him in the eye. "It aggravates my sinuses."

"I know it does."

"We'll fix this, Jacob. We will. We just need a little time." Arlene sniffled. "This church is a family. You've always said that."

"And I meant it, Arlene." He sighed. "But you know what else I've always said? That I'd stay here in Pine Valley unless God gave me new marching orders."

"Yes, yes, and I've also heard your sermon about how God can answer our prayers in ways we don't expect, so you needn't recap that for me now, either. That's all well and good, but I have to say, I really don't see much of the Lord in this, Jacob. What I do see is way too much Digby Markham." Arlene flung her crumpled tissue into the trash and got to her feet. "And *he's* not God, no matter what he may think to the contrary. Now, I've got some phone calls to make, but don't you pack one more thing in those boxes, do you hear me? Although it wouldn't hurt my feelings if some of this stuff found its way into the garbage. It sure would make dusting in here a sight easier. I don't see why you want to keep all that silly clutter, anyway."

Left alone in his office, Jacob studied the shelf in question, crammed full of lopsided Sunday school creations given to him over the years by a horde of small children.

Children who already had families of their own, and for whom good old Pastor Jacob was mostly a see-you-at-church-next-week kind of a relationship.

A three-legged turtle kind of relationship.

Maybe Arlene had a point. Maybe there

wasn't much on that shelf worth carrying with him when he left.

Because maybe—hopefully—depending on what Natalie had to say today, he might be needing room for a four-legged turtle or two.

The force of the hope that hit him alongside that thought startled him. He only knew one safe place to take feelings that strong. He closed his eyes.

Lord, You hold my life in Your hands. Whatever happens with this church and with Natalie, help me work this out in a way that honors You. But, Lord, if it's all the same to You, please...

"Jacob? Is this a good time?"

Natalie was standing in the doorway of his office, twisting her fingers together nervously. There was a stunned look on her face, and he winced.

"You ran into Arlene on your way in." He didn't bother to make it a question. He knew that look. He'd seen it on people's faces before.

Frequently.

"Yes. She seems pretty upset about your resignation, Jacob. Are you sure...really sure this is the right thing for you to do?" Her gaze wandered over to the empty boxes he'd lined up against one wall.

She was alone, he realized. "Where's Ethan?"

"I stopped in at Bailey's to drop off the

blueberries, and she babynapped him." Natalie smiled briefly. "I'm not used to being away from him. It feels weird, like I misplaced him or something."

"How's he doing?"

"Pretty good. Well, he's been really fussy this morning, but you know what?" Warmth sparkled into her eyes. "He actually laughed the other day. I was blowing raspberries on his tummy, and he laughed."

Jacob nodded. He was listening to her. He was. He was picturing the scene, a sweet milestone moment with Ethan that he was really sorry he'd missed out on. But he was also looking at her hair, drawn up into a high ponytail today. Pulled back so sternly, it emphasized the delicate lines of her face, bringing out an aspect of her quiet beauty that he'd never seen before.

He wouldn't have thought that was even possible.

But it was.

"Here." He gestured toward the chair Arlene had just vacated. "Sit down, and we'll talk."

She shook her head and stayed where she was. "That's all right. This isn't going to take very long."

And right then, he knew. The answer she was bringing him wasn't the one he'd been hoping for.

"You're moving back to Atlanta."

Natalie swallowed hard, then nodded, miserably. "I think it's the best thing to do."

Jacob's heart sank. A thousand arguments came into his mind, and he squelched them resolutely. But there was one thing he had to say. "I know how much you wanted things to work out with Adam, Natalie. But are you sure about this? He doesn't exactly have the most dependable track record where you and Ethan are concerned."

"Adam?" She blinked at him. "Adam has nothing to do with this. He left yesterday not long after you did. I have no idea where he went, or if we'll ever see him again, to be honest. He said he'd stay in touch, but…" She trailed off with a sad little shrug. "I know how Adam is. If we ever do hear from him, it'll probably be because he needs something."

Now it was Jacob's turn to blink. If Adam was gone for good… "Why are you leaving then? Have you thought about what we talked about?" He crossed the room, filled with an urgency to make her see, to make her feel what he felt.

The only problem was, he didn't have a clue how to do that.

Natalie took a small careful step backward as Jacob approached. She couldn't let him get close, couldn't smell that heart-tugging spicy scent of his. She had to keep her wits about her if she was going to get through this.

"Yes, of course I've thought about it." She hesitated. How could she make him understand? "You were right about what you said a minute ago, you know? I did want things to work out with Adam. I wanted Ethan to know his father, to have a real family, like I never did. But Adam just isn't cut out for the kind of life I'm hoping for."

"Adam's not the only man in the world, Natalie."

This was even harder than she thought it was going to be. More than anything else right now, she wanted to believe what Jacob believed, that this *could* work out. That somehow, some way, this could be *right*. For both of them.

But the last time she'd felt like this, she'd followed a pretty dream right into disaster. And her heart wasn't the only one on the line here.

So she shook her head. "Remember what you told me once? About how God answers prayers, but not always the way we want? Well, I never thought I'd say this, but I'm glad that Adam climbed out of that church window. Because if we'd gotten married, the whole thing would have been a disaster. Adam and I want very different things. And if you and I…" She paused, struggling to find the right words. After all, Jacob had never actually proposed to her. "…tried to be more than friends, it wouldn't work out any better."

He was shaking his head. "I'm not like Adam, Natalie. I want a family."

"I know. But that's not all you want, is it? Jacob, you might leave this church, although I'm not a bit sure that's really what you need to do, or even what you really want to do, for that matter. I think maybe you're letting your feelings about things cloud your judgment right now. Trust me, I know a little something about that. But even if you do leave, there'll always be another church. Won't there?" she asked, almost hoping she was wrong about the answer he'd have to give her.

She could see in his face that he was catching on to where she was leading him. He didn't like it, but he wouldn't lie to her. She saw the truth in his eyes even before he answered. "Yes. For me…yes. Always. I'm a minister, Natalie. I can't—"

"Change who you are." She finished the sentence for him. "Not even for somebody you care about. Neither could Adam. And neither can I. Your life is always going to revolve around church. Your work won't just be a part of your life. It'll be the focus of it. That's who you are,

Jacob. You never do anything halfway." She gave him a shaky smile. "I should know. So whoever you…choose to share that life with needs to feel the same way you do about your ministry, and I don't."

"You've had some bad experiences, sure. But I promise you, when you find the right congregation, it's different. It's almost like—"

"A family." She nodded slowly. "I know that's how you feel, and from talking to Arlene out there, it's pretty obvious that they feel the same way about you. That's one reason why I think you should reconsider leaving this job. But, the thing is, it's not how I feel, Jacob. I've just never experienced church like that. I don't think I ever will." She swallowed hard. "I know you're tired of being alone. I am, too. But take it from me, loneliness isn't a good reason to jump into the wrong relationship."

Jacob's face had lost color, and for once his eyes weren't twinkling into hers, teasing her to smile. He looked like he couldn't have smiled if his life had depended on it. "I don't know what to say, Natalie. I was ready to argue anything, promise you anything to get you to stay. But God called me into ministry a long time ago, and I've never doubted that call, not for a second."

She smiled at him sadly. "Nobody else doubts it, either."

There was a long silence. He seemed to be having some trouble saying whatever he had to say next. Finally, he spoke.

"But I do understand that the kind of life I've chosen isn't for everybody. I thought… I really hoped that God had put us together, you and me and Ethan. I'd started to believe that you and I were meant to be…a lot more than friends. But you're right. It's not fair for me to ask you to share a life you don't feel called to." He spoke quietly, but she could hear the pain in his voice.

This conversation was hurting him, and it wasn't doing her any favors, either. Besides, she'd already said everything she'd come here to say.

Except for one last thing.

"Goodbye, Jacob." Somehow a handshake didn't seem like enough, not after everything they'd been through together, so she tiptoed up to kiss him on the cheek.

At the very last second, he turned his head and met her lips with his.

Ever since Jacob had asked her to stay in Pine Valley, she'd wondered what this would be like.

Just as she'd expected, Jacob's kiss was just like Jacob himself. Gentle and sweet. Kind and strong.

Only one thing was different. Never in all

those daydreams had she imagined that this first kiss would also be the last.

She looked up into his face as he lifted his mouth from hers.

"Goodbye, Natalie. And may God's goodness and mercy follow you and Ethan, wherever you go and whatever you do, all the days of your life." He squeezed her arm once. Then he released her, went into his office and shut the door quietly behind himself.

Typical Jacob, Natalie thought as she stumbled blindly down the halls of the church toward the parking lot.

She'd left him with heartache and disappointment.

And he'd left her with a blessing.

Chapter Fourteen

A fever of 101 in an infant under the age of six weeks is considered a medical emergency.

Natalie's heart had been numb for two days, ever since she'd left Jacob in his office. But when she read that sentence in the baby care book he'd bought for her, it sprang instantly and painfully back to life.

She felt Ethan's hot head pressed against her neck. She had no idea what his actual temperature was, but he obviously had a fever. Now his fussiness and lack of appetite made sense.

Her baby was sick.

Natalie glanced at the old kitchen clock, ticking faithfully away on the wall. It was almost 9:00 p.m. on a Wednesday. All the doctor's offices in Pine Valley would be closed until tomorrow morning.

Could she wait until then?

Her mind drifted back over the past several days. The only sick person Ethan had been close to was Adam, and Natalie honestly hadn't figured that Adam would get near enough to his son to pass on a germ.

Obviously, she'd been wrong about that.

And Adam had gone to see Cora, and Cora was getting over the flu. Natalie didn't have to look in the baby book to know that the flu was dangerous for babies as young as Ethan.

Life-threatening, in fact. If there was even a chance that Ethan had the flu…

"That's it," she announced aloud to the empty house. "We're going to the hospital right now."

Five frantic minutes later, she was struggling to get through the front door, Ethan was wailing miserably in his car seat carrier, and she had his diaper bag and her purse slung over one shoulder.

Not that the purse was going to do her a whole lot of good, but she had all the money she'd made from the blueberries in there, at least.

Something wet splatted on her cheek and she blinked up at the sky. Of course. It was raining.

She heard a clatter of hooves and looked over to see Rufus climbing the porch steps. His wet fur glistened under the porch lights. She redoubled her efforts to wedge herself and everything she was carrying through the door.

The last thing she needed was for Rufus to scoot past her into the house.

Because if he did, he was just going to have to stay there until she got back, and goodness knew when that would be.

Unfortunately, like always, Rufus made it up on the porch in record time. He came toward her, tilting his horns curiously as he considered the half-opened door and the goat-sized gap between her leg and the door frame.

"Not now, Rufus," she said, her voice shaking. "Please, okay? Not now."

"Bleaah." Amazingly, Rufus stopped where he was. He watched as she locked the house, then trailed her calmly to the car. He leaned over and sniffed Ethan once when she set the carrier down to open the car door, but other than that, he didn't get in her way at all.

She hoped that wasn't the only amazing thing she could count on happening tonight. She also needed her sputtering little car to make it all the way to Fairmont Medical Center.

It cranked on the third try, and she breathed a grateful prayer. So far, so good.

She drove along the dark country roads as quickly as she dared, her heart thumping in anxious rhythm with the windshield wipers.

Her prayers seemed to be working until she

had to stop at her first intersection. Her car groaned, backfired twice and died.

Natalie pressed the gas and turned the key and prayed for all she was worth. *God! You have to make this car crank! Now isn't the time to play around! You know how sick Ethan is. You know that I have to get him to the hospital. Please. I need Your help!*

Nothing happened.

Ethan was still crying fretfully in the back seat, and every pitiful sob made Natalie feel more frantic. She had to help him. He didn't have anybody but her.

She leaned forward and peered through the rain running in rivulets down her windshield. She knew where she was. Jacob's church was just around that corner, but nobody would be there at this time of night. The buildings on both sides of the road housed small businesses, and they were all dark, locked up tight. There was no help to be found there.

She'd have to call somebody. She rummaged in the diaper bag for her cell phone, but cried out loud when she saw that it showed no signal. Cell service was always a little dicey in this small town, and the weather was making it worse.

God, what am I supposed to do now?

Ethan gave a coughing little sob. She couldn't just sit here. She'd have to walk until she found help. She pulled a little blanket, splattered with airplanes, out of the diaper bag. She'd drape that over Ethan's carrier to keep the rain out.

She left everything else in the car and started off down the street toward town with Ethan's shrouded car seat slung over one arm.

She could see the glimmer of reflected lights up ahead. Probably just streetlights, but she'd head in that direction, anyway. Maybe, just maybe, streetlights wouldn't be the only lights she'd see around that corner.

Please, let there be somebody still at work. Let there be a light on in one of the stores. Just one little light. Somewhere. Anywhere.

She rounded the corner, and as Jacob's church came into view, Natalie stumbled to a halt.

To her astonishment, the parking lot was jammed full. In fact, more cars lined the street in both directions. A few vehicles were even parked on the lawn.

But more importantly, every single light in the building was blazing, throwing squares of bright, wonderful color against the blackness of the night.

It was the most beautiful thing she'd ever seen in her life.

Arlene Marvin met Natalie the minute she stumbled into the church foyer. Jacob's secretary scanned her bedraggled appearance with a lifted eyebrow.

"Well, something's wrong. What is it?"

"Ethan's sick," Natalie gasped. She'd run all the way from the sidewalk into the church. "I think it might be the flu, and I was trying to get him to the hospital, but my car died."

"Oh, you poor dear. And you're soaked through, too!" Arlene's bony arm was around Natalie's shoulder in a minute. "Don't you worry about a thing, you hear? It's going to be all right. You're here now, and we're going to help you." Arlene used one orthopedic shoe to poke open the big doors leading to the sanctuary. Natalie caught a glimpse of overcrowded pews, and she could hear several people talking at once. "All of you! Stop that fussing, this instant! We have an emergency. Jacob! Doc Peterson!" she bellowed. "We need both of you out here. Now!"

For Natalie, everything that happened in the next few seconds was a blur. Arlene pushed her down into a chair and shrugged off her own thick sweater to cover Natalie's shaking shoulders. "It's just the stress, dearie. Getting good and warm will help."

The congregation responded to Arlene's alarm by flowing out of the sanctuary in a chattering wave. Before Natalie could blink, she was surrounded by a sea of concerned faces. The high-ceilinged foyer echoed with voices. Somebody pushed a foam cup of hot, milky coffee into her hand, at least three people were stroking her arms and a portly, balding man was crouched next to Ethan, checking him over with the calm, competent air of a professional.

He glanced up at Natalie. His face was serious, but he gave her a reassuring nod. "You were right, ma'am. This little fellow is having some trouble getting his breath. He needs a trip to the hospital, but I think you've caught it in good time. I'll ride along with you and keep an eye on him just to be on the safe side. Who's going to drive?"

An immediate hubbub of offers began, and keys began to appear out of purses and pockets, but one voice cut through the chaos.

"I am." Jacob was shouldering his way toward her, his face set with such determination that his crowded congregation parted like water in front of him. He knelt down beside her and looked up into her eyes. "I'm driving you, Natalie."

It wasn't exactly a question. But Natalie nodded anyway, sweet tears of relief springing to her eyes as she breathed a silent, thankful prayer.

She wasn't alone anymore.

Everything was going to be all right.

* * *

"How are you two doing back there?" Two days later, Jacob shifted his truck into its highest gear as they passed the Fairmont City Limits sign on their way back to Pine Valley.

Natalie's eyes met his in the rearview mirror, and she smiled from the back seat. "We're doing fine." Jacob smiled back, and their eyes lingered on each other an extra second before he was forced to turn his attention back to the road in front of him.

Natalie looked thinner, and there were shadows under her eyes that he didn't much like. But now that Ethan was well and truly on the mend, Natalie would perk back up, too, like a drooping rose after a spring rain.

He intended to make it his business to see that she did.

And then they were going to have another talk.

Because everything was different now. Things had changed, these past few days in the hospital. They'd sat together next to Ethan's bed, kept vigils during the nights and fetched each other coffee from the nurses' station.

Ethan had never been in any serious danger, but Natalie had hovered over him anyway, like a mother cat with one ailing kitten. At one point, when she'd made a move to get up from her chair to pace the room for the umpteenth time, he'd reached over and silently taken her hand in his own, keeping her where she was.

She'd looked over at him, and he'd smiled at her. And to his amazement, she'd smiled faintly back at him and settled back in the chair with a tired sigh.

And she'd left her hand nestled in his.

They'd stayed like that as the big institutional clock on the wall had counted away the night hours with its loud ticks, as the nurses and techs came quietly in and out to check Ethan's vitals.

Neither of them had said a word. Yet somehow, by the time the doctor had ambled in on his morning rounds, and Ethan had been pronounced well on his way to recovery, Jacob knew without a shadow of a doubt that his whole world had shifted irrevocably on its axis.

These two were his people now. For always.

He and Natalie just had to work out the details.

One rather obvious detail in particular.

He darted another glance up in the rearview and saw Natalie gently slide a gigantic teddy bear wearing a lab coat and a stethoscope back across the seat. It was one of three oversize bears crammed back there, and he had a stuffed duck that played music, two dogs and something that might possibly be a llama piled in the front passenger seat.

His congregation had nearly bought out the gift shop. The local florists were doing a booming business, too. Natalie had donated all Ethan's flower arrangements to the oncology ward. There were too many to transport home in the truck.

That reminded him. They were almost back at Lark Hill, and he'd better warn her. "They'll have brought food to the house, you know. Casseroles, mostly. And soups. Probably some pies. It's what they do, whenever somebody's been in the hospital."

She didn't look perturbed. "That's kind of them. What we don't eat right away, I can put in the freezer. It'll be nice not to have to cook for a few days while I try to get the last of the blueberries picked."

A few days? A few months more likely. She'd have at least one covered dish from nearly every family on the roll. Arlene would have seen to that. "I don't want you worrying yourself about those blueberries, or anything else for that matter. You know what the doctor said. You need to get some rest or you'll likely end up with the flu yourself."

"I hate to let them go to waste, though. Besides, Bailey's counting on them. She especially wants to make a good impression on that restaurant supply company that's buying them from her. I don't want to let her down. She's been so nice—" Natalie's protest faltered to a stop as they pulled into the bumpy driveway. "What in the world?"

The dilapidated little farm was swarming with people. Cars and trucks were parked crookedly throughout the yard, and there was a big table set up on the front porch, spread with enough food for an army. It was being guarded by elderly Lois Gordon, who was shooing Rufus away from a tempting chocolate layer cake.

"Get on, you pesty creature! Scat!" She flapped at the animal with a red-checkered napkin. "Will somebody *please* come get this goat?"

Nobody paid her any attention. The rest of his congregation, sporting bandannas and straw hats, were dispersed in the back field, baskets and plastic pails looped over their arms.

"Jacob?" Natalie had turned in the truck seat, craning her neck to see through the window. "What's going on?"

"They're picking your blueberries." Jacob couldn't stop the grin that spread over his face at the sight.

"Oh my," Natalie breathed as he pulled the truck to a stop. "Jacob, did you—"

"I had nothing to do with it. This is all them."

"They're here!" A cry went up as the truck was noticed. By the time he and Natalie had Ethan's carrier unfastened, Arlene had stalked up, her face grim with purpose. The congregation trailed after her.

"I'm glad you're back," Arlene announced as soon as she got within earshot. "Because we have a few things to get sorted out."

"Just let us get Ethan inside and settled down first." Jacob gestured at the sleeping infant.

Arlene didn't bat an eyelash. "Bobbi? Take that sweet baby, will you?" A blonde young woman stepped forward obediently. "It's all right," his secretary added, when Natalie made a little noise of protest. "She's a registered nurse. She'll put the little one down for you, and make sure everything's just right. And anyway, what I have to say won't take a minute. Jacob, we're refusing your resignation. We want you to stay on as our pastor."

A murmur of agreement immediately started, and Arlene made a shushing noise. "I'm not done. After you all left for the hospital on Wednesday night, Digby showed up at the church. He was running late for the meeting because he'd had a bit of news. Turns out that Digby's nephew was just hired on to be the pastor of Holy Fellowship Church over in Fairmont.

So of course, Digby plans to move his membership there."

"Wait a minute." Jacob narrowed his eyes at Arlene. "Isn't some third cousin of yours on the board of a big church over in Fairmont?"

"Well, yes. But that isn't important right now. What matters is that Digby's resigned from our board, and the rest of us have voted to put the fellowship hall project on hold for the time being. It was getting out of hand, anyway. Did you see the estimate for those tacky chandeliers Digby picked out?" Arlene shuddered. "We do want to build one eventually, mind you, but we're willing to wait a bit, if you feel that's best. And when we do go forward with it, we promise to keep it nice and simple. Isn't that right?" She shot a sharp look around, and heads bobbed in agreement. "So, there you go. Everything's all settled, and we can just forget that nonsense about you resigning. Can't we?"

Another pleading babble of voices broke out, but Arlene quelled them with a glance. The group settled into a tense silence.

Jacob looked over his smudged and sweaty congregation. He didn't think he'd ever seen them all together in their work clothes before. He felt a renewed surge of affection for these earnest, kind, sometimes frustrating people.

He wanted to stay.

But still. He glanced at Natalie, who was still looking over the blueberry-stained crowd with awed disbelief.

"I'm afraid I can't say yes or no right this minute, Arlene."

"Why ever not? It seems simple enough to me. You've said all along that this church is a family. Well, families have their spats, but they don't give up on each other. So? Are you staying or was all that just a lot of talk?" There was a telling little wobble at the end of Arlene's voice, but Jacob recognized the set of his secretary's bony chin. She'd dug in her heels, and he wasn't getting out of this yard until he gave her some kind of answer.

So he gave her the only answer he could. He reached over and took Natalie's hand in his. "I'm going to need to talk to Natalie first."

There was a collective intake of breath around them. Abel Whitlock chuckled.

"So, *that's* the way it is now. I figured as much."

"That's the way I *hope* it is. We still have some things to iron out." He looked down into Natalie's startled eyes and tightened his grip on her hand. The people crowded around them faded into a blur. "Natalie? I wasn't exactly planning to do this today, but I—"

"Jacob Stone, you stop right there!" Arlene's voice cut through the moment like a machete.

Jacob watched the sweet wonder in Natalie's eyes cloud, and he turned furiously on his secretary. "Arlene!"

The older woman stood her ground. "Don't you *dare* propose to that poor, sweet girl right here in front of all these people! What on earth are you thinking? Good grief, don't you ever plan out *anything*? Proposals are supposed to be romantic. And *private*. Even I know that much. Come along, the both of you."

Before Jacob knew what was happening, Arlene had her fingers clenched tightly around their arms, hustling them toward the nearest building.

She shut the door of the goat barn firmly behind them and stationed herself outside. "Now." Her voice was muffled by the wooden door. "There you are. It's not fancy, but beggars can't be choosers. That's what you get for not planning ahead. And Natalie, I wouldn't blame you a bit if you turned him down flat. Men!"

Jacob was almost afraid to look down into Natalie's face, but when he did, his heart swelled with relief.

She had one hand jammed against her mouth, her eyes were squeezed nearly shut and she was trying mightily to stifle her laughter.

"Sorry about all this," he whispered to her, but he wasn't. Not really. He'd never seen Natalie giggle like that before, helplessly, her shoulders quivering and her eyes twinkling with mirth.

Joy looked good on her.

She couldn't speak, but she nodded, waving away his apology with one hand. "It's all right," she managed to gasp finally. "They're all...amazingly sweet, really. I still can't believe they came out here to pick all those blueberries for me."

"Why, of course we did." Arlene's voice came clearly through the weathered barn door. "You're part of the family now, aren't you? And that's what families do. They stick together. *Right, Jacob?*"

"Arlene." Jacob raised his voice, but he didn't take his eyes off Natalie's. "Move away from the door, please."

"Oh, come on. I can barely hear *anything.*" Arlene fussed as she edged a miniscule distance farther away.

"At least Arlene and I agree on one thing. I wouldn't blame you if you turned me down flat, either. You were right the other day, Natalie. I *will* always be a minister, and there'll always be another church. If it's not Pine Valley Community, it's likely to be another one just like it. If you take me, my ministry is part of the package."

"I'm kind of a package deal, too, Jacob," she reminded him.

"If you're talking about Ethan, I couldn't love him more if he were my own son." He gathered both her hands in his now, praying for the right words to say. "But I know how you feel about church, Natalie, and—"

"Oh, I don't know," she interrupted him softly. "I think maybe church, one particular church, anyway, might be growing on me just a little."

He smiled. "Good to hear. But still, I understand that this is my calling, not yours. You'll always have the freedom to decide how involved you want to be in what I do. I want you to know that."

"I appreciate that. And Jacob—" Natalie began.

"There's more, and you'd better let me say it before I lose my nerve." He took a deep breath and tightened his grip on her hands. "My work demands a lot of me. There'll be times when I'll be elbows deep in somebody else's crisis, when my ministry will take up a lot of my time and attention. I'll always owe a part of myself to whatever congregation I'm serving. But I promise you this—you'll have all the rest of me, Natalie. You'll possess that part of my heart that nobody else even comes close to. In fact—" he traced the soft curve of her jaw with a gentle finger "—you have it now, you and Ethan. You'll have it always, no matter how you answer me today." He paused. "So, there it is. That's all I had to say. Except… I love you, Natalie. Will you marry me?"

"Oh, Jacob." Natalie pressed his hand against her cheek. "A heart like yours is plenty big enough for me to share with a church or two. Besides, I don't really have much choice, do I? Because I love you, too. And—"

"She just said she loves him." They could hear Arlene's stage whisper from outside the barn. There was a questioning murmur from the crowd. "Of course he's not down on one knee. Don't be ridiculous! He's in a barn, and he has his good pants on!"

Natalie's tremulous smile sputtered into giggles, and the sweet seriousness of the moment dissolved. Jacob threw an exasperated look in the direction of the barn door, but since he still held Natalie's hands in his own, he couldn't be too angry with Arlene. "I'm sorry. She means well."

"I understand." Natalie's laughter faded into a gentle smile. "And I know I'm not the only one around here who loves you, Jacob. Far from it. But from now on, I plan to be the one who loves you the best. And the longest. Of course I'll marry you."

"We have a yes!" Arlene's triumphant announcement to the crowd outside was greeted by a cheer, immediately followed by a shriek of dismay. "Lois! That goat has his dirty nose stuck in my layer cake! I spent all the morning on that thing. You were supposed to be watching him! Do I have to do *everything* myself?"

"I've got news for you, Arlene Marvin. That goat is *impossible* to deal with! And anyway, I don't see why I got stuck minding *your* cake. If it's so important to you, maybe you should look after it yourself!"

The sound of the two older ladies squabbling came clearly through the door.

"Don't you think you'd better go out there and tend to that before it gets out of hand?" Natalie murmured as Jacob tugged her closer.

"Nope," Jacob answered, not taking his gaze from hers. "This time they're just going to have to figure things out for themselves."

Then he leaned down and covered Natalie's smiling lips with his own.

Epilogue

"Cora's going to be here any minute to pick up the key." Natalie watched as Jacob tamped more dirt around the base of the wobbly fence post. "Do you think you'll have the pen fixed?"

"Yes." Her husband of two weeks gave the post one last wiggle. "But honestly, sweetheart, I don't think it's going to make much difference. Abel was right. Rufus can get out of any fence we put up."

"What are we going to do with you?" Natalie directed that question to Rufus, who flicked an ear at her from behind the fence. "You can't move to town with us, and I couldn't find anybody willing to adopt you. If you don't behave yourself today, Cora won't let you stay here, either."

"Natalie—" Jacob began, but he was interrupted by a short blast from a car horn. They turned to see a silver sedan pulling to a stop in front of the house.

"She's here." Natalie put up a nervous hand to smooth her hair. "Come on, let's go talk to her. And Rufus, for once in your life, please. Stay *put*."

When they reached Cora, she was standing beside her car, looking at the farmhouse. She spoke without turning her head. "My word. I haven't been out here in years." She sighed. "This is harder than I thought. My Ed and I argued so often about this old farm. Now that he's gone, I wish I hadn't been so stubborn about it."

The sadness in the older woman's voice settled Natalie's skittish nerves. Cora wasn't so intimidating after all. She was just another woman who'd made mistakes and had her share of regrets.

Natalie stepped away from Jacob's protective embrace and slipped her arm around the other woman's waist. "Here's the key, Cora. Why don't we go and take a look at the inside together?"

Cora looked surprised, but she nodded. "I'd like that. Congratulations on your marriage, by the way." She shot Jacob a narrow look. "I must say, you certainly didn't waste any time."

"Three and a half weeks from the proposal

to the ceremony," Jacob replied cheerfully. "I think that's a Pine Valley record."

"Well, you needn't boast. It's barely decent. You'd have raised a few eyebrows if people didn't already know how hasty you always are with your decisions, Pastor Stone."

Jacob glanced at Natalie, and his polite smile spread easily into a genuine grin. "There was nothing hasty about this decision, Mrs. Larkey. When something's right, you know it."

"I suppose," the older lady responded doubtfully. "Well, let's get this over with."

Their tour ended in the kitchen, and Cora trailed a finger along the countertop. "I'll give you credit, Natalie. You've certainly kept the house nice and clean. It needs a good bit of repair work, though. I'd no idea the place had gotten so run-down."

Jacob cleared his throat. "Are you still planning to sell?"

Natalie sent him a pleading look. They'd already discussed this, several times. Jacob needed to live in town, close to their congregation and his work. Lark Hill Farm was too far out to be a practical choice for a busy minister.

But Jacob knew how much she'd loved living on the old farm. No matter how often she assured him that she'd be perfectly happy in the pretty cottage they'd rented in town, or pointed out how much more convenient it would be when she started taking classes at Fairmont Community College this fall, he remained unconvinced. Just this morning, she'd caught him totaling up figures on a legal pad, trying to figure out a way to buy Lark Hill for her.

From the frustrated look on his face, he hadn't managed it, but that didn't matter to Natalie. Her heart had overflowed with a gratitude that bordered on disbelief. Jacob wanted so much to make her happy.

He didn't seem to realize that he already had.

"Yes, I'm planning to put the farm on the market." Cora was saying absently, "In fact, Bailey Quinn's already made an offer. It's not quite up to market value, but I'm inclined to accept it. Miss Quinn is all in a dither about those blueberries Ed put in. She says she wants to market them exclusively from her little store, and she even talked about making up a special label for them. Lark Hill Blueberries." Cora cleared her throat gently. "I think my Ed would've... rather liked that. Let's take a look outside now, shall we?"

Outside? But that was where Rufus was. Natalie felt a tingle of apprehension. She'd better play it safe and make her plea now.

"Cora, when I came here, I found a goat in the barn. Is there any way he could stay until we find him a new home? We'll drive out and feed him, of course. And it would only be temporary." Hopefully.

"I don't see why not, as long as he causes no trouble." Cora reached for the doorknob.

Rufus causing no trouble? Not likely. Natalie sent a frantic prayer upward. *Lord, You've already done so much for me. You've given me a man and a marriage beyond my wildest dreams, and I'm very thankful. I feel bad asking You for anything else, but Jacob tells me that You really don't mind. So, if You would please make Rufus stay in his pen until Cora leaves, I'd sure appreciate it. Amen.*

They were halfway across the backyard when it happened.

Rufus came barreling around the barn, headed straight toward them.

Oh no! She couldn't let Rufus anywhere near Cora, not after the way he'd flattened Adam.

"Jacob!" Natalie called frantically. Her husband, who'd lingered behind to answer a call, dropped his phone in the dirt and sprinted across the yard. Before he could collar the goat, Cora turned and caught sight of the animal racing in her direction.

"You! Stop right there!" the old lady thundered. Startled, Rufus skidded to a stumbling halt, ending up just inches from Cora's leg. He looked up at her, his yellow eyes wide.

Cora considered him without changing expression. "This is the goat you were telling me about?"

"Yes," Natalie admitted miserably. "That's Rufus."

Rufus craned his neck to nibble on Cora's slacks. Cora tapped the animal smartly on his nose. "Behave yourself! Those are new." Rufus backed up a pace, and she nodded approvingly. "Good boy. That's better." She rummaged in her pocketbook and unearthed a package of peanut butter crackers. "Here," she said, holding one out. "I imagine you'll find this tastes better than my pantsuit, you silly thing."

Natalie finally found her voice. "I'm so sorry. We've fixed the fence, several times, but he just—"

"Gets out. Of course he does. Goats are herd animals. They don't like to be alone." She held out a second cracker, which Rufus accepted enthusiastically. "My father kept goats when I was a girl. They're fabulous animals."

"Fabulous," Natalie repeated. That wasn't exactly the adjective she'd have picked, but she wasn't about to argue. She heard a muffled snort and looked suspiciously at Rufus. He was chewing contentedly on his cracker. The noise had come from Jacob, whose shoulders were shaking with suppressed laughter.

Natalie wasn't the only one who'd noticed.

"Are you laughing at me, Pastor Stone?" To Natalie's astonishment, Cora seemed more amused than insulted.

"I…" Jacob managed to say finally "…am merely rejoicing over the delightful surprises in God's creation."

"Mmm. I'm sure you are." Cora walked into the middle of the backyard, Rufus tagging along behind like an obedient dog. She surveyed the fields and pines around her. "What a lovely place this is," she murmured softly. "And what a silly fool I was." She glanced over at Natalie and Jacob. "I've changed my mind. I'm not selling. I'm getting tired of that retirement complex. There's nobody there but old people. Miss Quinn can lease the blueberry field, if she likes, and this goat can stay, as well. All he needs is a firm hand, and I'm just the woman for that. I might even get a few more animals to keep him company." Cora hesitated before adding, "And, to be honest, that's not the only reason I have for wanting to move here. I want you to know that I'm truly sorry for how my grandson and I treated you, Natalie."

"That's all forgiven and forgotten." Natalie glanced up at Jacob. "Besides, I think we can safely say that God's worked it all out for good, just like He promises to."

Cora nodded. "I'm glad you feel that way because I'd like the chance to get to know that little boy of yours. After all, he is my great-grandson. If you'll allow it, that is."

Natalie gave the woman an impulsive hug. "Of course, Cora. I'd love that!"

The older woman smiled, and some of the fretful wrinkles smoothed from her forehead. "We'll consider it settled then. And just so you know, I've already started depositing Adam's old allowance money into a college fund for Ethan. Where is the baby? I was so hoping to see him."

"Arlene's keeping him for us today." To everyone's surprise, Arlene had accepted their speedy marriage without the flicker of an eyelash and promptly appointed herself Ethan's honorary auntie.

"If you won't take a proper honeymoon, at least let me do some babysitting here and there. The two of you need some time alone before the rest of your little ones start coming along," she'd told them firmly. "Which I hope will be soon, by the way. I like a nice, big family for a minister. Keeps him humble and leaves him no time for causing his secretary any grief."

Natalie had laughed and agreed. So far, the arrangement was working out nicely.

And Ethan's fingernails had never looked better.

"Well, that's nice of Arlene, I suppose. I knew her back when we were in school. A fine, smart girl, but just between us, she was a bit bossy. Come along, Rufus. Let's go look at that barn of yours. It looks as if it could use some repairs." Cora drew in a deep breath of the spring-scented air. "Yes, I believe I'll move out here just as soon as I can arrange it. No sense waiting. It's just as you said about your marriage, Pastor. When something's right, you know it. Although—" she paused, lifting one thin eyebrow "—I must say, I'm amazed you got old Pastor Michaelson to go along with such a hasty wedding. I had quite a time with him over that first one. He's a fine minister, mind you, but he's grown awfully set in his ways. However did you manage it?"

"Yes, well." Jacob cut a glance at Natalie. She knew exactly what he was about to say, and their eyes twinkled together. "The truth is, he just happened to owe me a favor."

* * * * *

If you loved this story,
pick up the first book by
new author Laurel Blount,
A Family for the Farmer

Available now from Love Inspired!
Find more great reads at
www.LoveInspired.com

Dear Reader,

Hello! I'm so glad you found your way to Pine Valley, Georgia. If you read my first book, A Family for the Farmer, then we're old friends! If not, I'm so pleased you let me share A Baby for the Minister with you. Come sit down at the kitchen table, let me pour you a cup of tea and we'll get ourselves acquainted!

I'm a Georgia girl, so I feel right at home in this small town! It was wonderful to revisit some of the characters from my first story, and I enjoyed helping bachelor Jacob Stone find his very own happy ending. And I don't think the good pastor has anything to complain about, do you? After all, he didn't just end up with a beautiful bride, but he got an adorable baby son to boot!

Getting to know Natalie was a delight, too. She's a brand new Christian, still sorting through the mistakes of her past—and she's had some unfortunate church-related experiences that make her leery of Jacob's kindness. But with the help of the Good Lord (along with a bossy church secretary and a rambunctious billy goat), she and Jacob overcome all the obstacles to their happily-ever-after.

This story was such fun to write that I hope

these old Georgia back roads lead me to Pine Valley for another visit or two. In the meantime, I'd love to hear from you! Drop me a line at laurelblountwrites@gmail.com or come look me up on Facebook. I'm always ready for a chat!

Laurel

Get 4 FREE REWARDS!

We'll send you 2 FREE Books plus 2 FREE Mystery Gifts.

Love Inspired® Suspense books feature Christian characters facing challenges to their faith... and lives.

FREE
Value Over
$20

Get 4 FREE REWARDS!

We'll send you 2 FREE Books plus 2 FREE Mystery Gifts.

Harlequin® Heartwarming™ Larger-Print books feature traditional values of home, family, community and most of all—love.

FREE Value Over $20

YES! Please send me 2 FREE Harlequin® Heartwarming™ Larger-Print novels and my 2 FREE mystery gifts (gifts worth about $10 retail). After receiving them, if I don't wish to receive any more books, I can return the shipping statement marked "cancel." If I don't cancel, I will receive 4 brand-new larger-print novels every month and be billed just $5.49 per book in the U.S. or $6.24 per book in Canada. That's a savings of at least 19% off the cover price. It's quite a bargain! Shipping and handling is just 50¢ per book in the U.S. and 75¢ per book in Canada*. I understand that accepting the 2 free books and gifts places me under no obligation to buy anything. I can always return a shipment and cancel at any time. The free books and gifts are mine to keep no matter what I decide.

161/361 IDN GMY3

Name (please print)

Address   Apt. #

City   State/Province   Zip/Postal Code

Mail to the **Reader Service:**
IN U.S.A.: P.O. Box 1341, Buffalo, NY 14240-8531
IN CANADA: P.O. Box 603, Fort Erie, Ontario L2A 5X3

Want to try two free books from another series! Call 1-800-873-8635 or visit www.ReaderService.com.

---

*Terms and prices subject to change without notice. Prices do not include applicable taxes. Sales tax applicable in N.Y. Canadian residents will be charged applicable taxes. Offer not valid in Quebec. This offer is limited to one order per household. Books received may not be as shown. Not valid for current subscribers to Harlequin Heartwarming Larger-Print books. All orders subject to approval. Credit or debit balances in a customer's account(s) may be offset by any other outstanding balance owed by or to the customer. Please allow 4 to 6 weeks for delivery. Offer available while quantities last.

Your Privacy—The Reader Service is committed to protecting your privacy. Our Privacy Policy is available online at www.ReaderService.com or upon request from the Reader Service. We make a portion of our mailing list available to reputable third parties that offer products we believe may interest you. If you prefer that we not exchange your name with third parties, or if you wish to clarify or modify your communication preferences, please visit us at www.ReaderService.com/consumerschoice or write to us at Reader Service Preference Service, P.O. Box 9062, Buffalo, NY 14240-9062. Include your complete name and address.

HW18

HOME on the RANCH

YES! Please send me the **Home on the Ranch Collection** in Larger Print. This collection begins with 3 FREE books and 2 FREE gifts in the first shipment. Along with my 3 free books, I'll also get the next 4 books from the Home on the Ranch Collection, in LARGER PRINT, which I may either return and owe nothing, or keep for the low price of $5.24 U.S./ $5.89 CDN each plus $2.99 for shipping and handling per shipment*. If I decide to continue, about once a month for 8 months I will get 6 or 7 more books, but will only need to pay for 4. That means 2 or 3 books in every shipment will be FREE! If I decide to keep the entire collection, I'll have paid for only 32 books because 19 books are FREE! I understand that accepting the 3 free books and gifts places me under no obligation to buy anything. I can always return a shipment and cancel at any time. My free books and gifts are mine to keep no matter what I decide.

268 HCN 3760 468 HCN 3760

Name	(PLEASE PRINT)

Address	Apt. #

City	State/Prov.	Zip/Postal Code

Signature (if under 18, a parent or guardian must sign)

Mail to the **Reader Service**:

IN U.S.A.: P.O. Box 1341, Buffalo, New York 14240-8531
IN CANADA: P.O. Box 603, Fort Erie, Ontario L2A 5X3

HRCBPA18R

READERSERVICE.COM

Manage your account online!

- Review your order history
- Manage your payments
- Update your address

> ### We've designed the Reader Service website just for you.

Enjoy all the features!

- Discover new series available to you, and read excerpts from any series.
- Respond to mailings and special monthly offers.
- Browse the Bonus Bucks catalog and online-only exculsives.
- Share your feedback.

Visit us at:

ReaderService.com

RS16R